they

OF

Lawndale

Book 9 of the Kings of the Castle Series

Book 1 is the Introduction

Books 2-9 are standalones

Janice M. Allen

The Allen Group
Ridgecrest, California

This is a work of fiction. Names, characters, places, and incidents are products of the author's imagination or are used fictitiously and are not to be construed as real. Any resemblance to actual events, locales, organizations, or persons, living or dead, is entirely coincidental.

King of Lawndale by Janice M. Allen Copyright ©2019

Published by: The Allen Group (fka The Pernell Group), 943 E. 166th Place, South Holland, IL 60473

Trade Paperback ISBN: 978-0-9863149-3-3
Ebook ISBN: 978-0-9863149-2-6
Macro Digital ISBN: 978-1-7331782-7-3

www.janicemallen.com

All rights reserved. No part of this book may be used or reproduced in any manner whatsoever or by any means including electronic, mechanical or photocopying, or stored in a retrieval system without written permission of the author, except in the case of brief quotations embodied in critical articles and reviews. For permission, contact Janice M. Allen at janiceallen7519@gmail.com

Cover Designed by: J.L Woodson: www.woodsoncreativestudio.com
Interior Designed by: Lissa Woodson: www.naleighnakai.com
Editor: Lissa Woodson: www.naleighnakai.com

Manufactured and Printed in the United States of America

If you purchase this book without a cover, you should be aware that this book is stolen property. It is reported as "unsold and destroyed" to the publisher, and neither the author nor the publisher has received any payment for this "stripped" book.

KING
OF
Lawndale

Book 9 of the Kings of the Castle Series

Book 1 is the Introduction

Books 2-9 are standalones

Janice M. Allen

♦ DEDICATION ♦

To my real life King, Sammie Allen, Sr.,
and to my mom, Mary McCoy.

♦ ACKNOWLEDGEMENTS ♦

I thank God for life, love, health, and strength. I thank Him for the gift of creativity. And most of all, I thank Him for the gift of Jesus, my Lord and Savior.

To my husband, Sammie Allen, Sr., thank you for being so patient and supportive as I poured myself into writing this book. I love you more than you know.

To my mom, thank you for giving me more love than one heart can hold. Today and always, I love and honor you.

Much love to my editor, Naleighna Kai (Lissa Woodson), who kept me encouraged when I was ready to throw in the towel (more like ready to throw in the laptop :)).

Blessings to Karen Bradley. Your input was invaluable, my friend.

J. L. Campbell, thanks for laying eyes on my manuscript and giving your input.

Heartfelt thanks to my beta readers, Debra J. Mitchell and Ellen Kiley Goeckler, who made sure my story was on point.

And thanks from the bottom of my heart to everyone who purchased my books. Blessings!

CHAPTER 1

Could this entrepreneur and self-proclaimed community activist and child advocate also be a child abuser?

The airplane window reflected the damning words and photo that glowed on the screen of Dwayne's laptop. He reached up and adjusted the nozzle on the overhead airflow vent, but it did no good. His body would need to be frozen in a block of ice to offset the angry heat rising within him. And even that probably wouldn't be enough to melt his fury.

He skimmed the text splayed on the screen.

A family court judge ordered Dwayne Harper to attend parenting classes for physical abuse of a minor over whom he'd been granted guardianship and full parental responsibilities.

Laying his head against the seatback, he stared up into the ceiling. "They're going to pay for tarnishing my name with these lies," he whispered, trying to ascertain whether he could levy a lawsuit for slander or defamation.

A tall, slender flight attendant stopped next to his row, balancing a tray on her arm. "Here's your drink, sir."

Dwayne lowered the lid on his laptop. He knew the story on the screen was fabricated, but the woman smiling suggestively at him wasn't aware of that fact. Neither was anyone else who might catch a glimpse of the post and his photo.

The flight attendant reached past the man asleep in the aisle seat and handed Dwayne a miniature bottle of Tanqueray and a plastic cup containing ice and some tonic. "Can I get you anything else?"

He nodded toward his uncle. "Just some pretzels and water for when he wakes up." Dwayne lowered the man's tray table and read her name tag as she laid several tiny snack packs and a bottled water on it. "Thanks, Erica."

When she was several rows past him, Dwayne opened his laptop and adjusted the zoom down to seventy-five percent before clicking on another link his "almost" fiancé, Tiffany Richards, had emailed to him. An identical post popped up on a different Facebook page. He clenched his teeth.

Dwayne had opened Excel Charter School on Chicago's Westside three years ago. During that time, he had had to work his fingers to the bone to maintain a decent amount of social media exposure about how Excel was positively impacting kids whose potential had been overlooked and underfed in public schools. But it had only taken a half hour for over a thousand people to comment on this scandalous post. And only about a dozen had come to his defense. He shook his head.

Scrolling down the page, he read a few heart wrenching things people were saying.

> *I wouldn't be surprised if it was more than just physical abuse. He probably sexually abused that girl too.*

> *God don't like ugly. Folks get a little money and influence, and they think they can do anything and get away with it.*

I say put him in jail and let the inmates do to him whatever he did to that poor kid.

Dwayne took a couple sips of his gin and tonic, then tapped the elbow of the man napping peacefully beside him.

"Read this," Dwayne said, turning the laptop toward his uncle after the man's eyes opened.

Uncle Bubba stretched, rubbed his eyes, then pulled a pair of owl-rimmed glasses from his shirt pocket. As his gaze swept across the screen, he frowned with each sentence.

"They're publicly accusing me of abusing a child," Dwayne complained in a course whisper.

His uncle took his glasses off his smooth brown face and laid them on the empty seat between him and Dwayne. "Calm down, boy. I know that's not who you are. Everybody in the Lawndale neighborhood knows it. And those kids you mentor sure know it."

"Sanchez is behind this." Just saying the man's name made the hair on Dwayne's neck stand up.

Alderman Eduardo Sanchez had been accused of trying to bribe a couple of State Charter School Commissioners to deny Dwayne's renewal application even though Excel had met all the qualifications. Sanchez was acquitted of the charges because there was no clear evidence linking him to the crime and because he had the judge in his back pocket.

While Excel had narrowly escaped having its charter revoked, having been sanctioned on a warning list had done almost irreparable harm. The school was operating in a limited capacity at the moment. Dwayne was still mired in the appeal process for a full reversal of the District's decision.

Uncle Bubba tore open one of the pretzel bags, then unfastened his seatbelt as if his stomach would need extra space to accommodate the micro snacks. "If you think that man is gonna quit comin' after you, nephew, you better think again. You been in his crosshairs ever since you opened that new school. Especially after the people in the neighborhood cheered you on."

He popped several miniature pretzels in his mouth and spoke as he chewed. "Sanchez has stayed in office all these years by makin' promises to do this and that for the schools in his district, then sayin' it didn't get done because the State tied his hands."

Opening his water, Uncle Bubba took a swig before adding, "But then you come along and make him look real bad 'cause you raise enough money from the private sector every year to provide the nurses, social workers, and head docs at Excel that Sanchez only promises to put in the public schools in this district. You gotta understand what's really going on. That man thinks the people are gonna want you in office instead of him."

Dwayne mulled that over a moment. "You know that's the furthest thing from my mind, Unc." He turned the laptop toward himself and tapped a few keys to make the post disappear. "Educating young minds is my passion."

A flight attendant walked the length of the plane, stopping at each row to offer second helpings of snacks.

"Well, being one of the Kings of the Castle was the furthest thing from your mind too before you finally accepted the invitation to join them." He gave his nephew a pointed look. "Or did you forget that? 'Cause I can guarantee you Sanchez hasn't."

The Castle was more than just a magnificent edifice. It was a humanitarian organization founded by Khalil Germaine and comprised of individuals referred to as Kings. Each King had the power, resources, and global connections to affect positive change in communities worldwide. Unfortunately, the Castle's mission and reputation became tainted because a few Kings were intent on using their influence and the Castle's resources to feed their own insatiable greed for money and power.

Khalil had set out to clean house by recruiting new managing members to replace the crooked Kings. Scholars at the Macro International Magnet School he had founded in Chicago, provided a perfect pool from which to select new recruits to groom for the Castle. Dwayne had been one of eight boys Khalil mentored. Under Khalil's leadership, they were taught to have each other's back like brothers. They had grown up, gone their separate ways, and made their marks in the world before it was revealed to them that Khalil's mentoring had been geared toward preparing them to take their thrones at the Castle.

"That Castle and your brothers are a powerful bunch," Uncle Bubba said, repositioning himself as a heavyset man in a shirt threatening to pop all of its buttons squeezed down the aisle. "And now add the Knights into that. He should be afraid. From what you tell me, Sanchez's position in the Castle is on shaky ground 'cause he ain't upholding the standards."

The Knights were a younger group of men employed at Jai's health center. The Kings were now mentoring them to handle issues that plagued their communities.

"Sanchez knew what the Castle stood for when he agreed to be one of its managing members and didn't hold up his end of things," Dwayne replied. He wiped condensation off his plastic cup. "If he's about to be tossed out, he doesn't have anyone but himself to blame."

Uncle Bubba reclined his seat a little. "Don't matter. He's still ticked that somebody, especially a newcomer like you, is replacing him and all of those men who did such ugly things under the cover of darkness."

Dwayne reached for his laptop case under the seat in front of him. He opened it and pulled out a tattered flyer that had a picture of him alongside a white man in a U.S. Immigration Customs Enforcement uniform. They were shaking hands in front of the restaurant area of Excel.

The man in the photo was Dwayne's college roommate Teddy Styles. A few months earlier, Teddy had been unlucky enough to have his face shown in a CBS news story about the incident where, in one day, ICE agents arrested some seven hundred undocumented workers in food processing plants in Mississippi.

The flyer Dwayne held showed Teddy's picture from that news story as well as the image of Teddy and Dwayne outside Excel.

"Remember this?" Dwayne asked Uncle Bubba as he sat the paper on the tray table between them and tapped it. "It caused almost half of my Hispanic scholars and staff not to show up at school Monday and Tuesday of last week."

Uncle Bubba looked at it and let out a long, slow breath. "Neither one of us would've guessed in a million years that something like this would be on every windshield and light pole within five blocks of the school. Folks lookin' at this picture don't know you was just congratulatin' Teddy on his transfer to the ICE field office in Chicago."

Dwayne thumbed the edge of the paper. "I spent three whole days last week making phone calls and personally visiting my scholars and staff at their homes, trying to convince them that I wasn't helping ICE plan an immigration raid at Excel."

"Everybody workin' for you is legal, ain't they?"

"Yes, and so are all the scholars," Dwayne answered. "But some of them have undocumented friends and family. They were scared that if they were taken into custody, they'd be pushed to give up the identities and locations of the undocumented people they know."

When an older flight attendant with frizzy red hair came down the aisle holding a plastic bag open, Uncle Bubba brushed pretzel crumbs off his tray table and into a napkin. He tossed the napkin, pretzel wrappers, and empty bottle in the trash bag.

Dwayne realized that the moment the plane landed he would need to put in a call to his King brothers and get some advice on this personal attack being launched against him. Each one of them had professions and intelligence that would help him formulate a plan. He had done the same for them when issues arose in their lives that required all hands on deck. Dro was the fixer; Daron was the tech guru and inventor; Vikkas, an international lawyer; Jai, a doctor; Grant, a commercial architect; Kaleb, an award-winning property developer; Shaz, a family and immigration lawyer; and Reno, the owner of a domestic violence shelter. These men had become family when they reconnected after an attempt had been made on the life of their mentor, Khalil.

"Well, nephew, you can't let Sanchez mess up the kids' chance for a better life just because he can't stand to see nobody succeed but himself."

"It must have been people like him that Aung San Suu Kyi was talking about in *Freedom from Fear* when she said, 'Fear of losing power corrupts those who wield it.'"

Uncle Bubba nodded. "Yep, he's desperate 'cause he's a drownin' man."

"And I'm just the man to tie a weight around him so he'll sink to the bottom where he belongs."

CHAPTER 2

"You promise not to hurt any of the kids, right?" Chanel Bordeaux asked. Layers of silky dark hair were piled atop her head like a crown, accentuating her high, regal cheekbones. She stepped into the six-inch Jimmy Choo sandals laying beside a midnight blue crushed velvet sofa.

"I can only give you my word that I won't kill any of them," Eduardo Sanchez conceded. "But if I have to get rough with the students to get Dwayne Harper's attention, then that's what I'll do. Whatever it takes, I'm making sure he never gets that school fully reopened."

Sanchez paced the floor, running his freshly-manicured fingers across a thirty thousand dollar Rolex Sky Dweller. "And I want that managing membership seat he has at the Castle. He has no idea how much power it holds or what to do with it."

He grabbed a wallet off the coffee table. The heftiness of it and the designer label were both reminders of his financial prowess and all the under-the-table deals he'd brokered to make it happen.

"I love how you fight for what you want," Chanel said to her lover. She pulled a compact and Givenchy lipstick from a Prada clutch purse, and intensified the color on her garnet lips.

Always decked out in designer wear from head to toe, the two of them were a perfect match. The fact that he was more than twenty years her senior was a non-factor. Few men at age fifty-five could carry the swag he possessed.

He beckoned her to him.

Chanel took her time crossing the room, the fringe on the hem of her tight black dress swinging with each step. When she stood in front of Sanchez, he stroked a hand across the small of her back. "I could use your help in getting Harper out of the picture. He's a threat that I didn't take seriously at first. I do now."

She pushed back from him. "So is this why you're with me? To use my position on the State Charter School Commission to keep him so busy fighting to keep his school open that he won't have time to try to dethrone you?"

Sanchez shrugged. "You have a problem with that?" He traced the line of her chin then caressed her skin with his lips.

"No." She placed her hand over his. "Actually, I wondered what took you so long to ask for my help."

The man, and his connection to both students and their parents, were direct threats. One major difference about Excel was that it had a resource center for parents. In this center, parents had access to computers, help with resumes and job applications, and even a place to take online classes. The parents of each scholar were required to be part of creating their child's education and life plans, so they would then be aware of the part they needed to play to help their child achieve the goal. This resonated with people throughout Sanchez's ward. People couldn't get enough of sharing how their children were excited to learn again.

Instead of a cafeteria, Excel had a full-service restaurant that was open to the public in one area of the building. Scholars ordered their meals from the restaurant early in the day so their food would be ready when they arrived at the private areas during their designated full-hour lunch period. On Fridays, parents met in the school restaurant, which was run entirely by those scholars whose life plan included a career path in owning a restaurant or in hospitality management.

Dwayne Harper was positioning those students for success, but the fact that their parents were taking note in a substantial way was something that could come back to haunt Sanchez.

"So how much is this favor going to cost me?" he asked, pulling a credit card out of his wallet. He loosened the bow at the top of her low-cut dress and slipped the American Express card into her small, firm bosom.

Sanchez never had to pay to play when it came to women. He got any woman he wanted. None of them grew to be anything more than a short-lived fling, except in those uncommon occasions where the woman could offer something that helped further his crooked agenda. Chanel was one of those rare ones. For a woman like that, he didn't mind putting a little money in the game.

"My grandmother used to do that," he said with a smile. "I can't tell you how many times she lost something, thinking it was secure."

Chanel extracted the credit card out of her bosom and slid it into her purse. "I can tie his paperwork up in so much red tape that the new kids he wants to enroll will be great grandparents by the time he fixes all the problems I create."

"No, that's not enough." He kissed the hollow of her neck, followed by long, lingering kisses around her cleavage. "I need his reputation smeared too. I need you to get close to him. Find out some things about him. We all have skeletons in our closets, or at least a bone or two."

Chanel grazed her teeth across his neck, then breathed in his ear. "Get close to him, huh?" She curled her leg around his thigh. "This close?"

"Maybe not that close," Sanchez said in a low, throaty chuckle.

CHAPTER 3

Miguel Ramos didn't flinch as the man sitting before him in a three-piece suit stared him down. The teen squared his shoulders and walked up to the marble-topped oak desk that separated them. "What makes you think you can take people's money and then make them live like pigs just because they're old and don't have anybody to look out for them?"

Caesar Wilson waved Miguel off. "You'd better get out of my face, little boy." He turned his attention to shuffling through papers on his desk, not bothering to make eye contact.

Miguel cleared his throat and waited for the man with a dark complexion that matched those beady eyes to meet his gaze. "With all due respect, Mr. Wilson, I'm not a little boy. I'm sixteen. I'm about to graduate high school next year and go to college to study law so I can go after crooks like you." He pointed at the man who had caused his grandmother a world of grief, eyeing him with ill regard. For months now, he had pleaded with his father to allow his grandmother, who he called Abuelita, to come live with them, all to no avail. His father didn't want another mouth to feed, though Miguel's mother was the only one bringing in money and doing the feeding.

Caesar stapled a few of the pages he held. "This is grown folks' business and you don't know anything about it."

"You must be crazy to think you can get away with treating my grandmother and the rest of these seniors like this," Miguel shot back. "They pay you way more than that fleabag they live in is worth. And what do they get for their hard-earned money? Absolutely nothing." He slammed his hand on the desk.

Caesar visibly blanched, but quickly recovered with a smug smile. He motioned for Miguel to continue.

"They live in apartments that have no working stoves and refrigerators. Some of the doors are falling off the hinges because neighborhood thugs keep breaking into the units. But you just keep hiding out"—he gestured to the elaborate furnishings in the room—"here in your high class office, collecting the rent and leaving your tenants to fend for themselves. That ends now. Your rental properties aren't fit for human habitation."

Caesar Wilson's lip curled with disdain. He aimed steely eyes at Miguel. "Don't come in here flinging those ten-dollar words at me. My obligation as landlord is to provide them a place to stay as long as they pay their rent."

"Illinois law says it has to be livable," Miguel countered. He inhaled deeply to tamp down his frustration. "Their apartments are barely fit for a dog, let alone a person. Does your place look as bad as theirs?" He smacked his forehead. "Oh wait, I forgot. You live in one of those fancy high-rises downtown."

"Where I live is none of your business," Caesar ground out.

"I bet you wouldn't be able to keep living there if the rent from these rundown apartments stopped coming in, would you?" Miguel folded his arms across his chest.

Caesar's hands balled into fists atop the desk. "Are you threatening to keep my tenants from paying me?" His tone was low but deadly.

Miguel narrowed his eyes and matched the man's tone. "I'm saying that I know you received the list of demands I sent to you. I have the Fed Ex delivery confirmation to prove it."

Caesar opened a desk drawer and retrieved an unopened Fed Ex envelope. "You mean this?" He ripped it open, pulled out its contents. Reaching around to the side of his desk, he rolled out a small shredder and fed the pages into it without giving it a glance.

"Do whatever you want with the papers," Miguel warned over the buzz of the shredder. "But know this—if you don't see to it that those repairs are taken care of in the next thirty days, the tenants will use their rent money to get them done."

Caesar laughed, causing Miguel to bristle with anger. He placed his elbows on the desk and tugged on the cuffs of his heavily-starched shirt. "Let them withhold their rent and see if I won't throw them out on the streets." Steepling his fingers under his chin, he added, "Had some other tenants try that same nickel-slick trick. I took them straight to eviction court."

Caesar stood, but didn't match six-foot Miguel's height. "Now, did I like the fact that for the few months it took to go through the eviction proceedings they lived in my buildings without paying me? Nope, not at all." He fixed those lifeless eyes on Miguel. "But when the sheriffs showed up to kick them out of their apartments, it more than made up for that."

Miguel tracked the man's movements as he stepped around the desk, took three long strides and posted himself directly in front of Miguel.

The slumlord mimicked the sound of a crying baby. "They were boo-hooing and pleading not to be evicted because they had no where to go. They didn't have any family to take them in, and my building was the only place they could find to stay."

He rocked on the heels of his designer shoes, then leaned in so he and Miguel were a mere two inches apart. "It didn't make me no never mind, though, because I don't take to people trying to get over on me."

"But it's okay for you to get over on everyone, right? Especially people who have no other options," Miguel said, his mind teeming with thoughts of his grandmother. He affectionately called her Abuelita, which means "dearest grandmother" in Spanish. He often shortened it to just Lita.

How excited Lita had been several years ago when she became one of the first to have her Serenity House application approved. Serenity House promised to be like no other because it was backed by a Christian founder and supposedly established along Christian guidelines. The guidelines Caesar Wilson followed were based on greed alone.

Miguel pressed on, even though he worried that the things he had learned in studying ways to help his grandmother were not going to work on Caesar Wilson. "How long do you think Pastor Cordell and his wife are going to keep believing your lies? You saw them and New Calvary as easy prey. Here they were struggling to keep the doors of the church open because most of their members were seniors with little to no money to support the church's three mortgages."

Caesar grunted and looked down his nose at Miguel.

Determined not to back down, Miguel continued. "Many of them were just one Social Security check away from losing their places. You convinced them that God had called you to partner with New Calvary in providing affordable housing for the seniors in their congregation."

A flush of color rose up from Caesar's neck. "The Cordells saw my offer for what it was—an answer to their prayers." He pulled his shoulders back as though bracing for the next onslaught of accusations. "Now, they had a seasoned businessman willing to use his own funds to build senior housing for the congregation, and it would require no money from the church."

"Which would have been a good thing if you had honored your word," Miguel countered. "But you put the church's members in housing you would never think of living in. And when those same members started complaining to you, then threatened to tell Pastor Cordell that the way you were conducting business was smearing his good name, you went on the offensive and paid off the mortgages on the church and on the Cordells' home."

Miguel put a few inches between them. The man's anger was tangible. Miguel had listened to a few of the church members and found that whenever the Cordells got wind of their friends' complaints and brought it to Caesar Wilson's attention, he'd casually bring up that if it wasn't for him, they'd still be worrying about losing their own home. The same way he told the seniors that if it wasn't for his building, they'd be out on the street.

"Keep on mouthing off," Caesar warned, walking back to settle in his chair again. "Your grandma will be the first one without a roof over her head. And I won't even take her to court first."

CHAPTER 4

Dwayne and Tiffany jolted to a stop when their shopping cart collided with another. "Are you okay, baby?" he asked her.

"You must be stalking me," snapped Perry Richards, the husband Tiffany was still in the process of divorcing after three years of going back and forth to court. On the day their papers were to become final, Perry went before the judge and confessed that he had not been truthful about his income. He presented the first of many documents detailing assets he had tucked away, at Tiffany's expense, all throughout the marriage.

Originally, the judge had awarded Perry alimony along with half of Tiffany's pension and part of her savings, even though Tiffany had proven that she had financially carried the weight of the marriage all those years. By law, the soon-to-be-ex was entitled to it because she at the time was more financially stable. She even agreed to walk away from the house she had before they were married, because she had made the mistake of putting his name on the deed, which also entitled him to half of that as well. He lived there now, and she had an apartment because he refused to leave. They were at Home Depot choosing new blinds and area rugs for her place.

Dwayne had offered his place, saying he would get an apartment. She declined and said that she only wanted to be living in his home when she was his wife, and they were able to fully consummate their friendship and make it an intimate relationship. Dwayne's choice on the latter was because he did not want to be intimate with a woman who was not joined with him in holy matrimony.

With Perry's surprise confession, the divorce proceedings hit a stall—which was his plan overall. Now Tiffany was in a major holding pattern, waiting for all of the new documentation to be provided and reviewed. The judge also mandated for the property to be sold, even though Tiffany said Perry could have it free and clear just to get it over with so she could be free. Perry insisted on waiting for it to sell, then did everything in his power to run away all interested parties.

Perry Richards glared at Dwayne and Tiffany, then repositioned two cans of paint in his cart, then removed the box of light bulbs that the paint had crushed. He shook the box. Shards of glass rattled around inside. "Seeing you three times in one week, Harper. What are the odds?"

The overall-clad man laid the broken lights on the shelf, then gave the onceover to the items in Dwayne's cart. "What are you doing in Home Depot anyway? I heard you're no good with your hands." He looked in Tiffany's direction and said, "Ain't that right, honey?" as a smirk spread across his broad face.

Dwayne returned Perry's sly smile. "Guess me being in Home Depot is no stranger than me seeing you in the bank this morning, even though we all know you don't have any money. Or me seeing you buy condoms in Walgreens the other day, when anybody can look at you and tell that you don't have any skills in that department."

Perry's eyes bucked wide. He seemed momentarily stunned, like he wasn't prepared for Dwayne to have a comeback.

Glancing at his watch, Dwayne added, "Excuse us. We have places to be." He took Tiffany by the hand and went to push his cart.

Perry angled his in such a way that it blocked them from leaving.

Tiffany moved closer to Dwayne, hooking her arm around his.

Dwayne leveled a warning glare Perry's way. "What is your problem?"

"My problem is you thinking you're better than me because *my wife* is with you now." He sneered at Dwayne.

"Soon to be ex-wife," Dwayne corrected. "Would've been my wife by now if you didn't keep hanging on like a leech that doesn't know that it's had it's fill of blood. You've drained her for years and now that she refuses to give more, you're pissed that she's finally had the courage to wash her hands of you."

The diamond ring that Dwayne had given Tiffany the morning before going into court to finalize everything still remained on her finger because he refused to take it back. Whenever she felt at her lowest point in all of this, all she had to do was look at her left hand and remember the promise that the best was yet to come. That little directive had come from Milan, the wife of one of Dwayne's King brothers. Tiffany had been to the Castle several times to meet with the other eight women and Khalil Germaine, Dwayne's mentor. They had become close, almost like the family she never had.

"All you did was come along and pick up the trash that I sat on the curb." Perry's beady eyes leered at Tiffany.

Dwayne put his arm around Tiffany's waist and guided her to stand behind him. "Perry, you're an angry, ignorant man. Maybe even drunk," he said, sniffing the air around him. "But know this." He lowered his arm from his fiancé's waist and stepped up to Perry, eyes blazing holes through the man. "If you say anything else about her, I will drop you where you stand."

"Please, let's just go, Dwayne," Tiffany admonished, nudging his arm.

"Come on, Harper. What you waiting on?" Perry asked, his voice getting louder with each word.

People nearby took care to keep a safe distance as they passed by the crazy man who was acting a complete nut in public.

"Ain't nobody scared of you," Perry bellowed. He took two steps back, fists balled up at his side. "You want to be Mister Big Man. Step to me. Come on."

Dwayne waved Perry away. "I don't have time for this. You can stay here and act a fool all you want to. We're out of here." He took Tiffany's hand, left the cart and walked past Perry.

Dwayne froze in his tracks when a hand grabbed his bicep. Eyes fastened on his upper arm, Dwayne growled, "You're going to want to let go of me, like right now."

Instead of heeding the warning, Perry dug his fingers in Dwayne's skin.

Like lightning, Dwayne gripped Perry's wrist and twisted it so hard that Perry landed on the floor.

Perry squealed with pain, but then anger took over and he tried to snatch hold of Dwayne's leg. When a man wearing a tag that read "Manager" came down the aisle, Perry loosened his grip. He scrambled to his feet, holding his aching arm.

"Is there some trouble here?" the man asked, his face a mask of concern.

Perry pointed at Dwayne. "He's threatening me. I was minding my business and he just started yelling at me for no reason at all. Then he hit me. Call the police. I'm pressing charges."

Dwayne nodded toward the ceiling. "Look around, Perry. They have cameras all over the place."

The manager frowned, scratched his head, and said to Perry, "With all due respect, sir, yours is the only loud voice I heard. I was five aisles over and heard every word you said."

Dwayne moved to his shopping cart. "We'll just pay for our things and be gone, sir."

"I appreciate it," the manager said, extending his hand for a shake.

Perry didn't try to hide his disgust. "So now y'all all buddy-buddy?"

The manager said, "Sir, I'm going to have to ask you to leave or I *will* call the police on you."

Perry stuck his tongue out, swiped his thumbs across it, then held up his fists—or put up his dukes, as the old-timers would say. "I'd like to see you try to make me leave. I'm a paying customer just like everybody else." Bouncing around on his tiptoes, he threw phantom punches and ducked imaginary blows.

"This man is off his meds," Dwayne said, pulling a set of keys out of his pocket and was about to walk away when Perry slapped them out of his hand.

This had been a trying week. First the circus that Eduardo Sanchez's smear campaign had created, and now he had to deal with this clown. Dwayne merely chuckled and stroked his chin, knowing that he was going to give this man exactly what he'd been asking for.

Looking at the store manager, Dwayne said, "Make sure you remember every single word I'm about to say because I'll need someone to verify to the police that I gave this warning." He bent over and picked his keys up, then stood and looked at Perry, who was breathing fire.

"Perry Richards, I'm a black belt in karate. I'm required by law to tell you that before I mop the rest of this floor with your wide ass."

Perry responded with a snort.

Dwayne's remaining words were served up with a dose of venom. "If you touch me again or if you say another bad thing about Tiffany, I'm going to break your—"

Perry drew back to throw a punch at Dwayne's head.

Tiffany jumped out of the way.

In one smooth move, Dwayne swerved his head, brought his knee up, and snapped his leg out. His foot connected with Perry's jaw.

The man fell backward, his butt hitting the ground and the back of his head banging against one of the toilet bowls on display. He slumped to the right, the side of his face coming to rest on the open seat of another toilet.

"You had it coming," Dwayne warned as he dropped the lid down on Perry's head.

"You're so bad," Tiffany said to Dwayne, stifling a giggle.

"He'd just better be glad the plumbing's not hooked up. Otherwise, I would have flushed it until he drowned."

CHAPTER 5

Eduardo relaxed in an iRobotics heated massage chair and scrolled through the NASDAQ, Dow Jones, and S&P 500 indexes on his phone, strategizing how to best place his latest investments in the stock market. He could easily afford to blow his funds on the eight-thousand dollar chair, partly because of his successes in the market. A fair amount of his gains came from his innate knack for hedging his bets.

That's the exact tactic he was taking in his assault on Dwayne. A one-pronged approach had the potential to take Dwayne down, but it wouldn't ensure that he would *stay* down. On his quest to destroy Dwayne, Eduardo minimized his risk of failure by attacking on multiple fronts. He was most proud of the latest strategy he had implemented a few weeks ago.

He pressed his legs and back against the chair to feel the full effect of the massage rollers moving up and down his body. Folding his hands behind his head, he closed his eyes and re-lived the day he put that plan in place. Dwayne Harper would never see it coming.

* * *

Eduardo sat in the back seat of a minivan, content that the tinted windows kept his face out of view. He'd rented the vehicle for this particular errand, knowing that his silver Lamborghini would have attracted too much attention.

At exactly half past three, teenage boys of all shapes and sizes came out of the Excel Charter School. The place covered an entire city block. It had been built more like a glass and steel office building than the typical red brick school. The way Dwayne connected with the adults showed how brilliant he was. Eduardo Sanchez had every intention of dimming that brilliance down to a dull shine, or extinguishing it altogether.

A few of the students roughhoused with each other. Several crowded around one boy's phone, pointing at the screen and giggling.

"Probably looking at some naked girl," Sanchez muttered.

"They ain't doing nothing you wasn't doing at that age," his right-hand man, Franklin, said from the driver's seat.

"I'm still doing it. The difference is that I know what to do with a female when I get her. Just ask that boy's mama." He pointed toward Miguel Ramos, who was coming out of the main entrance of the school. The words "All Scholars Are Welcome" were on a sign above the door. "I had her and she didn't even know it."

"What you mean?"

"Her name's Rosa. She worked at this hole-in-the-wall Mexican food restaurant," he answered. "And ooo-wee was she fine! A friend took me there, and I almost didn't go because it was way below my standards. But I wanted to cut a deal with the man, so if some greasy spoon was where he wanted to seal the deal, so be it."

He laid down the newspaper he'd been skimming through. "After I saw her, I went back to that place at least twice a month, even though I couldn't stand the food. I tried everything to get her attention—flirting with her, complimenting her, telling her boss what a great worker she was."

Taking a handkerchief from his suit jacket pocket, he wiped away the faint trace of newspaper ink that stained his fingertips. "She acted like she didn't hear a word I said. I knew some women played hard to get, but this woman was on another level. I had to have her just because she said I couldn't."

Frank locked eyes with Eduardo in the rearview mirror. "So what happened?"

"I lucked up about three months later. I went to the diner one day when it had been robbed. The guy had put a gun to Rosa's head because he caught her trying to call 911. She was so shaken that after the police came and left, the boss told her to go home early."

Eduardo recalled the sight of the woman wrapping herself in a thin coat, scarf, and gloves, intent on walking home in below-zero weather. "The thieves had taken the customers' and employees' wallets. She didn't have money to catch a bus or cab."

"So, you had to give her a few bucks before she gave you some loving?" Franklin snickered. "I thought you didn't pay for it, either."

"Nothing of the sort," he said, miffed that Franklin would say that. "She left on foot, then came back a few minutes later looking like a popsicle." He cracked a small smile. "I overheard her asking her boss to advance her a day's pay so she could get a cab because there was no way she could walk four miles to her house on that day. When he couldn't because the robbers took everything from the register and cleaned out everyone's pockets and jewelry, it was a little easier for me to sweet talk her into accepting a ride home that day."

Closing his eyes, he savored the memory. "I bought her a hot chocolate to go—told her it was to help her thaw out. After she was in the car, the ice on the windows made it hard for her to see me slipping something in the cup while I walked around the back of the car."

The powder had no taste and no smell, but it would put her out of commission for a few hours or so. And that's all the time Eduardo had needed.

Eduardo let loose with a heavy sigh. "After she drank it and passed out, I drove to a dead-end street and had my way with her in the back seat." He cracked the window a bit to counteract the heat suddenly flowing through him. When he was through with her, he fixed her clothes, waited for her to wake up, then started tapping her cheek and saying things like 'What happened? You said you felt dizzy, then you passed out. Has this happened before?'

"When I finished putting on my act, I took her home, helped her to the front door, and drove off."

Franklin looked at him through the rearview mirror. His expression turned dark. "Thought you said you never forced a woman. Women threw themselves at you."

"She wanted it," Eduardo protested, shifting a little in the seat. "I just helped her get to that decision quicker."

"So that boy, Miguel, that you've been talking about is yours?" Frank's gaze landed on the teen.

"Yes." Eduardo leaned forward, tapped Franklin on the shoulder, and pointed. "He's crossing the street now. Take a good look at him when he crosses in front of the car."

Franklin lowered the sun visor and put on his dark shades.

When Miguel had walked several feet past the car, Eduardo said, "Now do you believe me?"

Franklin nodded, taking in the fact that the teen was nearly identical to the man in the rear seat. A younger version, but identical all the same.

"I had no intention of returning to that restaurant," Eduardo confessed. "That is, until the businessman who took me there in the first place wanted to close another deal. And he chose that same place."

Eduardo motioned for Franklin to head home. "I pretty much knew that the drug I had used would cause Rosa's memories to be fuzzy. So even if she thought she recognized me when I went back to the restaurant, I could easily brush it off and say she was mistaken."

"Did you ask her out again?" Franklin asked, his tone less judgmental than it had been.

"I'm too smart to push my luck like that. But after the meeting when I went to the register to pay the bill, I saw a baby picture on the wall that looked just like it could have come from my mother's collection of baby pictures. I asked whose baby it was. The man gave me my change and then pointed to another picture of the baby and its mother. It was Rosa Ramos."

Franklin maneuvered around a slow-moving garbage truck. "Why do you care about this boy anyway? You're the one always saying you'd never have any children and you'd never claim any of the ones the women try to pin on you."

"That's still true. But you know how I operate," Eduardo countered. "I'm going to always keep something on my radar if I think it might come back to bite me. I've had people keeping me abreast of what the boy does, who he hangs with, who and what's important to him. And you wouldn't believe who he's close to."

Franklin gave him a blank stare through the rearview mirror.

Eduardo smiled. "Let me put it this way: Miguel will be a good ace-in-the-hole for me to use against his mentor, who is none other than Dwayne Harper."

CHAPTER 6

"I can help you around all that red tape so you can keep your school open," a sultry voice purred. "

Dwayne looked up from the bean and cheese burrito he had just taken a bite of. "Well if it isn't Miss Bordeaux," he said.

Chanel batted her smoky eyes ever so slightly at him. "Please call me Chanel," she said, pulling out an empty chair at the table where he sat hurriedly eating lunch at The Veggie Grill in the heart of downtown Chicago.

"May I?" she asked, glancing down at the chair.

"I guess so," he replied, wiping his mouth with a napkin and pushing his tray aside.

"I know two of the three people who keep opposing you," she said, gliding into the chair in queenly fashion.

"You're on the very same State Charter School Commission that is challenging my school. So why would I believe you of all people are going to help me?"

She flashed him a smile that made the bright sun outside look more like a candle. "Because I agree with you that we need your charter school."

Dwayne packaged up the rest of his uneaten meal. "Why am I finding that hard to believe?"

"I've read up on you." Her wide eyes captured his. "A lot of specialty schools boast about targeting a young person's talents to cultivate the best in them. You actually do that, but that's not what makes your school stand out. One big difference in your school's mission is how you teach them to collaborate for success, not to compete against each other."

Dwayne eyed her with suspicion, but he appreciated her observation. "I want to teach them that in this world, we can do more together than we can by tearing each other down."

Inwardly, Chanel kind of admired the man for what he was doing with this particular school. His genius came through in the fact that Excel was so state of the art and forward-thinking. She'd pulled several articles and one documentary dedicated to his work.

Dwayne had put a lot of thought into making Excel a reflection of the experience he had had at Macro International Magnet School when he was a teen. Khalil Germaine, the driving force behind Macro, had created it to be an environment that would not just inspire success, but that would incite a passion for it. Evidently, Dwayne Harper had that same passion. Khalil had said at the onset, that scholars cannot be taught the same. Everyone had a different way of understanding and processing. That also meant that they had a unique way of learning—some visual, auditory, written. Dwayne used a combination based on what the teens responded to best.

Like Khalil had done, Dwayne called the teens at his school "scholars" instead of students. The word was a reminder that they were more than any limitation the world tried to put on them.

The classrooms inside Excel Charter School were nothing like conventional ones. Each scholar's individual station was set up like an office, complete with a full desk, a leather executive chair, a Mac computer, supplies that rivaled any corporate outfit, and a private closet in lieu of a locker.

A cluster consisted of ten-to-fifteen of these stations grouped together in a large space called a boardroom. The scholars in a cluster studied together and collaborated on assigned projects.

They rotated roles according to a schedule. The same scholar who functioned as the cluster's president or chairman of the board today, would have his turn serving as the cluster's administrative assistant or custodian on another day. The idea was to give the scholars a feel for leadership and every aspect of owning a business—from top to bottom Dwayne knew that some of the best leaders are those who value everyone who contributes to their success, be it the custodians who keep the office toilets clean or the executives at the helm.

Though their studies were concentrated in blocks of various foundational courses that encompassed English, math, science and world history, the scholars were also required to participate in physical components including swimming, martial arts, military drill, and various forms of cultural dancing. Each scholar was taught about various forms of music—opera, jazz, R&B, world music. They were also required to pick two instruments to learn to play.

Another amazing offering at Excel was a half hour of mental preparation on how to take tests. Scholars were taught breathing techniques, meditation, focus, how to analyze the groupings of question, and other things that would lead to successful results. The students' test scores were off the charts and the public school sector was definitely taking notice.

Chanel's hand snaked across the table and gave Dwayne's hand a gentle pat. "I know I'm supposed to be 'the enemy' and 'the big bad wolf,' but your program has made me have a change of heart."

Dwayne slowly extracted his hand from under hers. "About charter schools?"

"Not all of them. Just yours. I'd like to see your technique in action."

Inwardly, he chuckled. "Well, in a few weeks, the scholars are hosting our first ever Gala at the Castle."

"Really?" she perked up. "Tell me more."

"They've been working on it since the school year started seven months ago. They're responsible for every part of the event. They budget for their particular area of participation, they staff it, they do all the event planning. Together. Each scholar gets three grades: one for their individual effort, one for their team's effort, and one for the success of the event as a whole. So, if the food was great but the service was lousy..." He raised his hands and shrugged.

"Is it too late for me to get a ticket?"

Dwayne mentally calculated things. "I know we had a certain amount set aside for VIPs, but you'll have to talk to Dylan to be sure." He flipped through his briefcase and passed her a business card. All of the scholars had one. "He's a junior at Excel. If I didn't know any better, I'd swear he had a hard drive in his head instead of a brain because this young man can keep more logistics straight than most computers."

"Maybe we can meet tomorrow to talk more about it?"

He twisted his mouth. "*We?*"

She nodded.

"Well, Miss Bordeaux, I won't have a free moment until after the Gala," he said, placing his leftovers into an eco plastic bag. "In addition to mentoring those scholars in my school, I teach ESL classes through the week."

"English as a Second Language, right?" Chanel chimed in.

"Exactly." He stood, aiming to put distance between him and a woman focusing way too much on his efforts.

She jumped up too. "Didn't I read somewhere that you also have a twin sister?"

Dwayne didn't answer because now, even more, he wondered what Chanel's end game was.

"She's a psychologist or something like that, right? Had some type of high profile case."

Dwayne's thoughts were flooded by a barrage of flashbacks of the situation Eduardo Sanchez had used to put him on the wrong side of social media. Dwayne's sister Val often added tasks to his calendar whenever she thought he had one unbusy nanosecond. Most of these assignments had to do with Hispanic clients of hers who could use an advocate outside of Val's counseling office.

He said to Chanel, "Just last month, my sister referred an immigrant client of hers to me because the lady was having a hard time understanding and navigating the system. She recently was unjustly sentenced by a judge to attend parenting classes."

"I think I read something about that. Why is that unjust?" Chanel said, first reaching for his hand again, then pausing as though she thought better of it. "Her name's Sophia or something like that, right? If she abused a child, she should be held accountable."

"That's just it. Sophia didn't harm the child," he protested. "Her husband did. And when she stepped in to stop him, he attacked her. Yet his lawyer somehow convinced the judge that his wife attacked him and provoked him to hit her."

"So you volunteered to accompany her to the court-ordered parenting classes? How noble is that?" Chanel crooned, beaming as though her statement presented wonderful news that benefitted her somehow.

The facilitator knew Dwayne was only there to support Sophia, but he asked Dwayne to sign the attendance sheet because he wanted to give him a certificate as well due to his consistent attendance and participation.

"The parenting class and the Gala both end a week from today, so I don't see myself being able to talk to you until then," Dwayne said.

"No worries," she said, and this time she splayed a hand on his chest. "I can wait as long as it takes."

Somehow, Dwayne got the feeling that this was a problem in the making.

CHAPTER 7

Tiffany scanned her last three years of tax returns. She was overwhelmed with the volume of papers required by the financial affidavit each party to a divorce proceeding had to resubmit to the court.

Being married to Perry Richards had not been easy. But divorce court was a destination she'd wanted to avoid at all costs.

Unfortunately, Perry took this to mean he could intentionally be the worst possible husband he could be, and there would not be a price to pay. But his actions and attitude over their five-year union caused their marriage to become rife with financial discord.

All this nonsense meant she had no choice but to miss a meeting at the Castle. Cameron, Daron's mate, promised to fill her in on things a bit later.

As she laid a stack of bank statements in the scanner's feeder, she recalled the day when one frightfully devious act on Perry's part bankrupted every remaining iota of love and compassion she had for him.

* * *

Layla Anderson parked in front of Tiffany's house. "Are you sure about this?" she asked Tiffany.

Tiffany gave her friend's fleshy hand a gentle pat. "Yes. I have to do this. I have to get my research and other work off the computer before he gets it in his head to delete it, post it online, or do something else vindictive like that." She had worked far too hard on the dissertation for her Doctors of Nursing Practice degree, and she wasn't going to let him sabotage it.

"Can I at least go inside with you?" She laid a hand on Tiffany's shoulder.

"No because I'm only going to be in there a for a minute. I'm not trying to get clothes or anything else. I can come back and pick those things up when I know Perry's not here."

Layla glanced at Tiffany. Her normally wide, jovial brown eyes were tight and worried. "If he wants to act crazy, at least there'd be two of us instead of just you by yourself. You could hold him down and I'd poke him in the eye real good," she quipped.

Tiffany knew her friend only wanted to coax a smile from her. But Tiffany didn't have it to give. The best she had to offer right now was a hug.

"Layla, you're like a sister to me and I know you'd do anything for me, even if it meant putting yourself in harm's way. But some things a person has to do alone, and this is one of them." She reached to open the car door.

"Before you go, can I ask you something?" She fingered a tiny sister-loc which hung around her neck like a necklace.

Letting go of the handle, Tiffany said, "Sure."

"Don't get me wrong. I'm not judging you or anything, but why did you stay with Perry so long? I ask myself that question over and over again because I just can't see myself sticking around to let a man keep treating me as badly as he treated you." She touched Tiffany's arm. "No offense, but I just want to understand why."

A thousand memories rolled through Tiffany's mind. The day Perry nearly tore down the bedroom door because they'd been arguing and she'd retreated there to keep from losing her mind over his vicious barrage. The many times she distanced herself from her friends and even her own family just to appease his irrational jealousy. The way he talked down to her in front of others in order to make himself appear bigger, better, brighter.

"Truthfully," Tiffany replied. "I never knew the reason why I stayed until today. I guess part of it was that I felt I had to honor the vow I made. A bigger part was that I hoped my love would change who he was. But the greatest reason is what I learned about myself after that stunt he pulled today."

Perry had told Tiffany's aunt that Tiffany ran off with another man and was in danger. He had known full well that Tiffany was actually visiting Layla's church and they'd be going to eat afterward. Yet, he had made a conscious decision to mentally and emotionally torture the woman who had been a mother figure to Tiffany by making her think that Tiffany was in grave danger and in her aunt's physical state, she was helpless to come to her aid.

"You know how much my aunt means to me," Tiffany told her friend. "She stepped in and loved me as a mother when my own parents were so busy climbing the social ladder that they didn't have any time for their only child."

Layla took a long slow breath. "I tell you what I would have learned if he'd done that to someone I loved like a mother," Layla said, reaching in the back seat for her enormous purse. She stuck her hand deep in the bag and pulled out a .22 caliber Saturday Night Special, a sheathed Buck Knife with a six-inch blade, and a personal flamethrower capable of shooting a stream of fire up to a foot-and-a-half away. "I would have learned how satisfying it would be to shoot him, stab him, and then set him on fire," she said, not so much as cracking a smile across her delicate caramel face.

Tiffany gathered her friend's arsenal and dropped the items back in her purse. "To answer your question about why I stayed with Perry," she said, "I couldn't leave until I knew I had the strength to stay gone."

Layla blinked twice and tilted her head. "Meaning?"

"If I had left after any of the other incidents, he would have been able to sweet talk me—"

"And guilt-trip you," Layla added.

"—into staying. He would have acted like he was ready to make a change, and that would have drawn me back to give it another try. But what he did today made it impossible for me to keep fooling myself about who he really is." She shook her head.

"How evil and cruel does a person have to be to call my widowed aunt, make up a phony cry no less, and tell her that the only person she considers as her child has gone missing and is possibly in mortal *danger? Anything could have happened to her by the time I found out what he had done and was able to let her know I was all right."*

She rubbed her hands down her face. "My aunt could have suffered a stroke or heart attack just at the thought that I had come to such a demise."

She wiped the tears that streamed from her eyes. "If anything had happened to that woman, I promise you I would've gone straight to prison because I would've taken that man out of his misery."

"So how do I know that you won't go in there now and do that? You don't know how you'll feel when you see him face-to-face. And you don't know how he'll act."

"But I have to do this alone." *Tiffany left the passenger seat of Layla's Kia Soul and peeked at Layla through the window.* "Just pray for me," *she said, then strode purposefully up the walkway to her two-story home.*

Then she whipped around and tipped back to the car. "But hand me that Saturday Night Special just in case."

Layla complied, then said, "I thought you said you only needed the Good Lord."

"Yes, but my folks are from Marshall, Texas. Where we praise the Lord and pass the ammunition. If Perry decides to act a fool, the Lord will direct the bullet on its path."

"Amen, sister," *Layla said, giving her a fist bump.*

Perry was right at the door when she stepped inside. Couch cushions were strewn across the carpeted floor. Their wedding pictures had been taken out of the frames and tossed about the living room. He'd had a meltdown, as he always did when things didn't go his way.

"Whew," he said, stepping aside and wiping his brow with the back of his hand. "I'm so glad you're home. I was worried sick." He glanced around at the mess in the room and said, "Just overlook this. I was a little upset."

Tiffany's mouth drew in and she glared at him, unblinking. If looks could kill, someone should have invited the coroner to the house.

"Move, Perry." She plowed past him.

Perry walked close behind Tiffany. "I didn't mean to make all those phone calls today, but I ... I was just worried about you, that's all."

She did an about-face. "You told at least two people that I ran off with another man. One of them was my mother. You made her think her only child had vanished from her life without a trace." Her brow furrowed so hard that she felt the onset of a headache.

Putting her hands on her hips, she asked, "Why did you tell that lie in the first place? You knew exactly where I was—at church with Layla and then going out to eat."

He pleaded with his eyes. "I don't like when you're not with me," he whined, rocking his burly body on the heels of his shiny shoes. "When I couldn't reach you on your cell, I started imagining all kinds of things happening to you, and I was going crazy because I couldn't protect you."

Tiffany rolled her eyes up to the ceiling. "We. Were. In. Church!"

she snapped. "Who do you know that answers the phone in the middle of Sunday service?"

"The pastor?" Perry joked. "Maybe it's Jesus on the mainline."

He reached out to touch her arm. She recoiled.

"Everything's all right now," Perry said. "We can get through this. Like all the other times." He folded his hands as though he was about to pray. "Pretty please."

The very fact that he had no trace of remorse for the panic he put everyone through was confirmation enough to Tiffany that it was time to get out of the marriage.

Marching past him, Tiffany went in the office, stuck a flash drive in the desktop computer, and transferred all her files to it.

Perry stood at the door and held his tongue while she was in the office. He couldn't do the same when she went in the bedroom and came back with her makeup case and a dry cleaner's bag containing clothes she'd picked up the day before.

He stood in the doorway, blocking her exit. "Will you do me a favor and stay with me tonight?" He raised two fingers in the air like he was ready to do the boy scout pledge. "I promise that when tomorrow comes, if you still feel like you need some space, I'll understand."

"Spending the night would be rewarding you for bad behavior. I'm through doing that," she said, her free hand chopping the air with the last few syllables.

For once in his life, Perry was speechless. Tiffany knew that only

God could close this roaring lion's mouth. Any other time, Perry's response would have been to force his will upon her, even if it meant having to verbally or emotionally attack to do so.

Tiffany breezed out of the front door, that Saturday Night Special still tucked into her bosom. Layla leaned across the seat and opened the passenger door.

Her friend's face was laced with expectancy. "You look ... I don't know how to describe it." She examined Tiffany's features. "What happened in there?"

Tiffany released a pent-up breath she didn't realize she'd been holding in. "I expected a huge blow-out, but there was none. It seemed like an angel kept Perry's tongue and anger in check just long enough for me to get my stuff and get out of the house safely."

Little did Tiffany Richards know, Perry kept calm because he was planning what would turn out to be a three-year firestorm.

CHAPTER 8

"How often did your husband hit you?" Dwayne asked Sophia, the woman his sister Val had asked him to help with legal problems. With all the issues surrounding his time accompanying her to the court-appointed classes, he needed a bit more clarity on her situation so he could ascertain where the Kings needed to get involved.

"Only when he was drunk," Sophia said in her broken English. "Or mad," she added, fidgeting with her wedding ring. "Or tired." She lowered her embarrassed gaze to her feet.

"So I guess we could say always," Dwayne surmised.

A nervous half-smile slipped past Sophia's defenses.

Sophia was enrolled in Dwayne's English as a Second Language class. She had shown up to the ESL class more than once with handprints around her wrists and bruises on her arms. He had pulled her aside after one class and asked if she was having problems at home.

She immediately denied it, but relented a second later. She was too afraid to go to the police. But keeping it bottled up inside was slowly killing her, so she eventually took him up on his offer to introduce her to someone she could talk to about her problems. His sister Val, a psychiatrist, had been counseling with Sophia for only several weeks when the woman found herself being crucified by a family court judge.

When Val learned of it, she asked Dwayne if he would consider being an advocate for Sophia while she dealt with her court case. The most important part would be accompanying her to court dates and parenting classes to ensure that the language barrier wouldn't prevent her from understanding or being understood.

Today was the day the three of them discussed this proposition together.

"How often did you hit your husband back?" Val asked Sophia in a quiet voice.

Sophia's eyes widened. "Never." She laid shaky hands on her lap. "Not before he slap our daughter. Then I hit his arm. Hard. He bleed."

"How could you make his arm bleed by hitting it?" Dwayne asked, noting her petite hands.

"Because it was already injured," Val answered. "She told me he'd been stabbed the night before in a bar fight. He needed stitches, but didn't go to the emergency room because he said they'd get the police involved and he didn't need that kind of trouble."

Dwayne slid forward in his chair as Val gave Sophia's hand a gentle squeeze.

"So what happened after you hit him?" he asked.

Sophia's heart-shaped face clouded over. "He drag me on the floor, force knife in my hand, and then scream, 'She stabbing me!' He scream so many time. Then he call 911."

"*He* called the police?" Dwayne asked, before he put his focus on Val for a moment.

"Si. They take us to the station." Her breathing hitched as emotions kicked in. "I beg them not to take me. I could not leave my daughter. She only three."

"But they took you anyway?" Dwayne asked.

She nodded, then wiped away tears and blew her nose.

"So here's the hard question," Val said, placing a hand on her shoulder. "I want you to take a moment to think before you answer it. What do you hope to gain from coming to these counseling sessions?"

Sophia pondered the question. She covered her mouth. Tears rolled down her face.

"It's okay, Sophia," Val said. "This is a safe place to say exactly what you feel."

Sophia lowered her hand, opening a floodgate of pain and disappointment that exploded out of her mouth in a blast of Spanish words. "Quiero entender lo que en mi corazón y mente hace quedarme con él. Me manipula. El me controla. Me devalúa. El me abusa."

Dwayne translated so his sister could keep up with the conversation. "She says she wants to understand what in her heart and mind makes her stay with him. He manipulates her. He controls her. Devalues her. Abuses her."

"That's a good start," Val said to Sophia, jotting down a note. "Anything else?"

Sophia held back her waterfall of tears long enough to share the remainder of her heart. When she had no more words, Val looked to Dwayne.

"She says she wants to learn to love herself—if that's even possible—so she can teach her daughter that she is worthy to be loved."

He settled back into his seat and looked at the women. "I have some people who are going to get to the bottom of things," he said. "And I'll continue going with you to those classes."

"I do not want to cause any more trouble for you."

"Don't you know?" he said with a grin. "Trouble is what I do best."

CHAPTER 9

"Do you think you can free up a copy of all the attendance sheets for the current session of parenting classes being held at your community center?" Eduardo asked Ontario Mills.

Ontario's smile widened and he shifted his beefy frame in the rickety gray office chair. He rolled it back a half inch and kicked his boots up on the shabby desk.

"Boss man, I could free up all the inmates in a maximum-security prison if you asked me to."

"I'm sure you could," Eduardo chuckled, gesturing to the row of corroded metal file cabinets behind Ontario. "But for now, I just need more of those attendance sheets with Harper's signature on them."

"No problem," Ontario answered, going to the file cabinets. "How soon?" He wrenched open a drawer and raked through the messy folders in it.

"Today. I need the most amount of people to see them in the shortest amount of time. Need to keep the pressure on Harper."

"You got it," Ontario said. "I'll just use those dummy profiles you had me set up. They can't be traced back to either one of us. I can even post cell phone pictures of him entering and leaving the class, too. When

I heard he was attending, I hid out in my car a couple evenings and snapped the pictures on the off chance that they would come in handy one day."

"You're always thinking ahead and looking out for my best interest." Eduardo walked over and clapped him on the shoulder. "That's why I pay you the big bucks."

"For sure, boss man," Ontario piped in. "What should the posts say?"

Eduardo leaned against the desk, mulling things over for a moment. And another thought came to mind. Ever since he'd put Chanel on to Dwayne, she'd been a little distant. He wondered if the man's do-gooder spirit was rubbing off on her. Dwayne was charismatic that way.

Eduardo and Chanel had been able to manipulate a few scenarios that had put quite a few dollars in their pockets. But her seeming hesitation at handling the Dwayne situation was a major concern. He couldn't have her going soft on him. She was a vulture, but in this instance, she couldn't seem to devour her prey.

"How about just showing more of those photos and sign-in sheets? You did a good job last time of making sure to mention that the sheets came from a court-ordered class for people charged with child abuse. Peoples' imaginations will have already filled in the blanks. Now that Harper's publicly disputing things, let's hit him with another round. This time with … receipts."

"That'll work just fine because if I don't know anything else, I know that folks who stay on social media all day just looking for dirt and drama don't care whether what they're reading or saying is true." He pulled out a manila folder. "They just want to have their say about any and everything. I guarantee they'll re-post and re-tweet so fast that the story will spread like the California wildfires."

"That's exactly what I want to see happen," Eduardo said, scanning the sheets Ontario handed him. "Make that perfect Mr. Harper have to spend so much time defending and rebuilding his reputation that he doesn't' have enough time to fight for that school of his or those students. Oh, correction—his *scholars*." He tapped the first few pages and slid them back. "I never want him in a position to even think about running for a political appointment."

Ontario took out his cell and took screen shots. "When we're done with him, he'll see how quickly folks can turn on you—even those you're trying to save."

CHAPTER 10

Eduardo Sanchez had never known his father. Nor had he ever had a desire to know the man. The streets had raised Eduardo. Everything he needed to know about life, he'd taught himself. More often than not, his mother had been missing in action, too. She had abandoned her son for whatever man was her latest lover. At fourteen, Eduardo found himself completely alone, having to scrape for everything he had.

So he had treaded lightly and planned strategically when it came to making Miguel need the father who'd never needed him.

Franklin, who'd continued to keep tabs on Miguel, found the perfect opening for Eduardo to slither into the boy's life. It didn't take much snooping around for Franklin to find a way for Eduardo to step in to save the day for his newfound child.

Seeing that Miguel visited a senior apartment building every day, Franklin had simply paid one of Eduardo's minions to show up there one day playing the role of a good son scouting out places for his beloved mother. The man asked Miguel's opinion and got an earful.

A day later, Franklin had returned, stopping seniors as they left or entered the building and asking if they recommended the place. Not only did he hear firsthand how despicable it was, but one of the residents took him inside.

The moldy smell permeating the hallway had made Franklin hold his hand over his nose. It had come from water that soaked the walls when the fire department battled a blaze that had broken out on the second floor. Mold and mildew had the perfect breeding ground when the landlord refused to pay to have the space professionally cleaned. Broken floorboards, mice droppings, shattered windowpanes, and the smell of something decaying in the walls completed the scenario.

These people's misfortune would be a jackpot for Eduardo.

Miguel had welcomed the offer when Alderman Eduardo Sanchez popped onto the scene telling the boy he wanted to help the seniors fight the slumlord. He was the one who had provided Miguel with research on Illinois landlord/tenant laws before the boy had his first confrontation with Caesar Wilson. He knew that it would light just enough fire to the wood that would force Miguel into a no-win situation. Eduardo had looked up Wilson's history and knew exactly how to play him.

Although Dwayne was Miguel's mentor, Miguel hadn't shared the housing situation with him because he wanted to impress Dwayne by showing him that he could solve a complicated problem on his own.

After Wilson received several fines for the condition of the building, Miguel began looking up to Sanchez. That was when Sanchez sprung the news that he was the boy's father. But he made Miguel promise not to mention it to his mother. He took a gamble with that, but the boy was so intent on proving that he could solve problems on his own, he complied.

Eduardo had done his homework. Miguel's mother had met and married a man when Miguel was five and his older sister was six. This man never bonded with Miguel. Never wanted to. He used every occasion to humiliate Miguel and his mother over the fact that she didn't know who her son's father was.

Dwayne had been a good positive role-model for Miguel the past few years. But being torn down in his home was slowly chipping away at who Miguel saw himself to be. The boy was ripe for the picking. And Eduardo was ready to reap the harvest.

After Eduardo told Miguel he was his real father, it took nearly a month for the shock to wear off. But Miguel found it a little easier to believe when one day Sanchez showed him his baby picture from forty years ago.

In time, the thought of being Eduardo Sanchez's son was easier to swallow. Especially since Eduardo didn't take the "I'm your father; do as I say" stance. Instead, he praised Miguel for everything he did and treated the teen as an equal, unlike Miguel's stepfather, who could find nothing good in him.

Having cultivated Miguel's mind, Eduardo began planting seeds of doubt concerning Dwayne Harper. At first, Miguel came to Dwayne's defense—vehemently. Sometimes, Eduardo felt that the bond between them was too thick to break. But after Eduardo dangled bit after bit of fabricated evidence in his face, Miguel started taking the bait.

Mission accomplished. In Miguel, Eduardo Sanchez had landed an even better inside track to Dwayne Harper. No better weapon against a powerful man, than someone he cared about.

CHAPTER 11

"Did those folks knockin' on the front door say police?" Uncle Bubba asked Dwayne, stepping into the living room holding a bowl of popcorn.

Tiffany was going in for a meeting at the Castle straight after work and had blown off Dwayne's attempts to drive her there. She must have thought he would pump her for information about the women's talks, because she had shown him that she could be as tight-lipped as the Kings could be in such matter.

Since he didn't have to take that drive to the Castle, he'd arrived at Uncle Bubba's house earlier and they'd just settled into the modestly decorated space to watch the Chicago Bears play the Green Bay Packers when a loud series of bangs snatched their attention.

Dwayne left his spot on the tan leather couch and parted the curtain just enough to get a peek outside. He turned to his uncle, who wore a robe and sweatpants—and who gratefully hadn't tipped over to the closet to grab his shot gun. "You heard right."

"Well don't just stand there, son," Uncle Bubba said, shooing him towards the entrance. "Open the door and see what they want."

Dwayne clicked open a set of locks and pulled the heavy wooden door open. "May I help you?" he asked the four uniformed officers who glared back at him as if he was wearing a t-shirt that said "cop killer".

"We have a search warrant," replied the one closest to the door. His right hand rested on the butt of his revolver.

Dwayne frowned, but didn't make any sudden moves. "For what?"

"Are you the homeowner, sir?"

"No," Dwayne said. "My uncle is."

"And where is he?"

Dwayne noticed the subtle movement the officer made as he unfastened the hook that secured his gun in its holster.

Uncle Bubba stepped up to the door. "I'm Paul Burgess. What can I do for you?"

"I'm Officer Greenly," one of the men replied in a curt tone. "We have reason to believe illegal immigrants are being held here against their will. We'll have to search the place."

Dwayne schooled his features into a neutral expression, though inwardly every fiber of his being wanted to slam the door on their faces for coming there with such an outlandish accusation. "Let me see that document."

The taller of the three men slapped a paper against the screen door. Dwayne perused the words on the page.

"Well, I can tell you now, ain't no illegal immigrants here," Uncle Bubba warned, pulling the belt of his robe tighter around his slender frame. "Never was."

"We'll see for ourselves, sir," Greenly snapped back, looking like he was ready to pounce on the old man who dared stand up to him.

Unlocking the screen door, Uncle Bubba said, "Come on in and do what you need to do."

The two of them stepped aside. The officers entered, the taller one pointing to where each of the other three should go. They spread out into the living room, adjacent dining room, and the office on the other side of the living room.

Hearing them opening and slamming the coat closet, drawers, and file cabinets, Uncle Bubba knit his brow and said, "Um, tell me again what y'all are lookin' for, Officer Greenly."

"Illegal immigrants."

"In the *drawers*?" Uncle Bubba's bushy eyebrows drew in. "Are they pocket-sized people?"

The officer stiffened, his face darkened with embarrassment. "Sir, we don't need any comments from the peanut gallery."

Uncle Bubba elbowed Dwayne in the side and whispered, "You ask me, they're the only nuts around here."

Dwayne nodded then pointed toward the officer leaving the office and heading down the hall.

"Greenly," Uncle Bubba said.

"Off-i-cer Greenly," the man said between gritted teeth.

Uncle Bubba waved away the man's correction, then nodded toward the hallway and said, "You better stop that one before he gets to the back bedroom."

Greenly's hand gestured for his fellow officers to hold their position. "Why? You've got something to hide?"

"Not at all. But those two babies in that bedroom back there just fell asleep after crying for two hours straight."

"Did you steal them from illegal immigrants?"

"Steal? No." Uncle Bubba sighed, shaking his head at their ignorance. "They're my grandchildren." Josette was Greta's grown daughter from her first marriage. Bubba claimed her as *his* child. No room for "steps" in his vocabulary. "We're keeping them all week so their mother can finish studying for her bar exam."

"Why can't their father keep them?"

"Not that it's any of your beeswax," Uncle Bubba retorted. "But he's a full-time firefighter, that's why. Plus"—his index finger shot up—" he's a chaplain at a hospital. He's supportin' that family by himself and payin' for her schoolin' out of his own pocket. The least me and Greta can do is step in and keep the kids this week. Our daughter is a genius. All she needs is to be able to concentrate on nothin' but that test, and she'll ace it."

"So where's your wife, since she's supposed to be keeping the babies?" Greenly narrowed his eyes as if he'd backed Uncle Bubba in a corner.

"Greta went up to the pharmacy to get their prescription."

Both babies had colic. Uncle Bubba and Greta gave every ounce of energy they had just to keep the two little ones comfortable. Josette had spent countless hours with the insurance company before they finally approved the medication the pediatrician said the babies needed. She had called her mother just before the police arrived to say the prescription was ready. Greta had slid out to pick it up because Uncle Bubba had already started making dinner once the babies finally were resting peacefully. Greta insisted Dwayne stay when he offered to go instead, because she wanted to scoop up a few more items as well.

Uncle Bubba leveled a glaring look at Greenly. "You boys can go on and finish up yo' searchin'. But if you wake up them two babies, be prepared to call yo' boss and tell him you ain't comin' back to the station today 'cause every one of you rascals is gonna be stayin' right here until you put both of 'em back to sleep."

Greenly looked at Dwayne, who shrugged and said, "I was stuck here until one o'clock Tuesday morning because I accidentally closed the door a little too hard. So, I'm telling you straight up … he's not playing."

Stepping into the hallway leading to the back bedrooms, Greenly gave a low-volume warning. "Ross, Marzetti, Whitehall, keep it quiet back there. And hurry up. I think this old geezer might seriously try to keep us here if the babies wake up."

Thirty minutes later, the cops filed into the living room. "All clear, sir," said a skinny, bald one.

Dwayne opened the front door and jutted his thumb toward the street outside. He shut it a half second before the last cop cleared the threshold.

The man made an abrupt about-face. From across the room, Uncle Bubba could see the officer's jaw tightening and the veins in his temple throbbing.

"Sorry," Dwayne said, holding back a grin. "Didn't mean to hit you."

"I should haul your—"

"Let it go, man," Greenly warned, grasping his cohort's shoulder and walking him off the porch. "Leave it be. Unless you're down for babysitting, 'cause I'm certainly not. I don't want to babysit my own damn kids. Let's go!"

Dwayne closed the door and pounded his fist against his palm. "Give me a second, Uncle Bubba," he said, reaching for the phone in his pocket. "I have to check into something." His footsteps rang out on the hardwood floor as he made a hasty exit to the office.

Uncle Bubba was in the kitchen taste-testing the collard greens simmering on the stove when Dwayne finally finished the call. "You thinkin' what I'm thinkin', boy?"

"That they weren't searching hard enough? They didn't find your shotgun."

"That, too, but I mean the other thing," Uncle Bubba shot back.

"I'm way ahead of you, Unc." Dwayne said, slipping his phone in his shirt pocket. "Sanchez is behind this."

"Exactly what I thought." Uncle Bubba forked up some greens in a small bowl and handed them over.

Dwayne pulled the bottle of Louisiana Red Hot from the cabinet. "I called my boys Daron and Dro. Told them what happened and asked them to look into it." He doused his greens with the fiery concoction. "That's why I was on the phone so long. They confirmed that this little mini-raid was Sanchez's doing."

"That don't surprise me none," Uncle Bubba said, putting the lid back on the pot and turning the burner off. He looked over Dwayne's shoulder. "Um, you think you've got enough hot sauce in that bowl? You're going to pay for that on the wrong end."

Dwayne put a forkful of greens to his lips and moaned. He swallowed them down. Uncle Bubba was great in the kitchen. Dwayne's domain was the grill. He took in another bite and said, "Daron and Dro found out that Sanchez called in a few favors to get a phony search warrant and to have some of the cops on his payroll pay us a visit."

Uncle Bubba shook his head.

Dwayne pointed his fork at his uncle. "Thankfully you didn't mention putting a bullet in one of the officers if they woke the babies."

The old man wasn't above saying that either. Lack of sleep can make folks do what they normally wouldn't do. And he hadn't had more than four hours of sleep per day since the babies came to visit.

CHAPTER 12

"I know I've said this more than once, but Dwayne is a really good man," Chanel said to Tiffany. Her expensive charm bracelets tinkled as she cut into a lemon cranberry scone and forked up a small piece.

Tiffany felt the familiar rush of anxiety that plagued her the first time she had been around Chanel. She and Dwayne had run into Chanel at Outback Steakhouse. Chanel had invited herself to join them. The woman sucked up to Dwayne with over-the-top flattery and flirtation. She harped on his drive to help youth and her dream of having a house full of children.

Somehow, Tiffany had let Dwayne talk her into taking this meeting to feel Chanel out because he didn't feel the need to meet with her alone. He wouldn't go into it more than that, but if Chanel was serious about helping with Excel, then it shouldn't require Dwayne's presence. *If* she was serious.

Tiffany had sent a text to Cameron to run a background check on Chanel Bordeaux before making it to this meeting. What came back was that the woman was fierce when it came to business and her entire career had centered around the same experiences as Dwayne.

Taking a deep breath, Tiffany silently talked herself off the ledge.

Don't let Chanel get you rattled. Dwayne loves you. No matter how beautiful, or smart, or well-connected Chanel is, Dwayne is in love with you.

Tiffany added cream to a steaming cup of hazelnut coffee and took a sip. "I don't have long to meet with you. I have to get back to work. Twelve-hour shift at U of C tonight. A nurse's work is never done." She took another sip. "What is it that you wanted to see me about?"

Chanel opened her purse, pulled out a photo and gently slid it on the table in front of Tiffany's hand.

Tiffany blew in her coffee cup as she glanced absently at the smiling pre-teen in the picture, whose features were only slightly familiar. "Who's this? A niece of yours?" She took another sip of the steaming liquid.

"Nope," Chanel said, examining her gleaming nails. "She's your daughter."

Tiffany's heart slammed against her chest. For a moment, the world swam in and out of view. "Wh-what are you t-talking about?" she stammered, taking a closer look at the image. The girl was the spitting image of Tiffany, with a couple similarities to the boy who had broken Tiffany's heart when she was just fourteen years old.

Her parents had thought they had the formula for raising the perfect child. Minimal communication. Constant critiquing. Little-to-no affirmation. They found out the hard way that to a naïve, attention-starved girl, the smallest compliment from a good-looking classmate like Damien Jackson seemed like a Thanksgiving feast. Hard for her, even harder for them when those compliments turned into shared homework sessions, which became stolen moments after school, and further into open thighs, followed by broken promises and a pregnancy neither one of them was prepared to handle.

A man rushed by their table, talking loudly into the cell phone glued to his ear. He almost tripped over a briefcase another patron in the restaurant had placed on the floor. The momentary distraction gave Tiffany a moment to gather her composure.

Chanel regarded Tiffany with a mixture of amusement and ill will. "I did some research on you." She tapped a finger on the photo. "It's amazing what you can dig up on a person if you have money and the right people in your back pocket."

"I don't have any children," Tiffany countered, forcing her eyes not to dart away from Chanel's intense stare.

"Of course not, because you gave her away and thought no one would ever find out."

"You don't know what you're talking about." Tiffany took a five out of her purse, laid it on top of the bill on the table, then stood. "We don't have anything else to talk about."

Chanel gripped Tiffany's hand to halt any movement. "If you don't tell Dwayne about her, I will."

Tiffany's heartrate took a nosedive. All efforts at denial went by the wayside. "You wouldn't."

"Try me," Chanel fired back with a self-satisfied grin.

She snatched away, then slid back into the chair she had just vacated. "What do you want from me?"

"Your man, that's all." She smiled, and the sight of it almost made Tiffany lose that wonderful breakfast that Dwayne had prepared for her. "I'm working on it. You'll soon be out of the way, since you really can't be his anyway."

"Dwayne?" The sting hit Tiffany so hard she could hardly breathe. She pulled her shoulders back and gathered what was left of her confidence. "He loves me. I know this from the top and bottom of my heart. Why on earth would he want you?"

"First of all, because I don't come with nearly the amount of baggage you do." Chanel looked at her with disdain, adding, "How long has he been waiting?" Her eyes crinkled with delight at Tiffany's obvious discomfort. "This man is fine. He's rich, and his entire life is centered around children—educating them, mentoring them. Any fool would know that if you give him a child of his own, you lock him in for life." She grinned and whispered, "I'm working on that, too. I can always tell when a man is tightly-wound and a woman hasn't been handling that"—she leaned over and lowered her gaze to Tiffany's lap—" kind of business."

Tiffany held off on speaking. Chanel had hit on a sensitive place in the relationship with Dwayne. He, an honorable man, would not have any intimacy between them until she was completely free to be his woman.

Chanel flipped the photo around in her hand. "This little girl right here is my ticket to that man's heart. He won't possibly want you when he finds out that you abandoned your flesh and blood, then lied to him. He's all about"—she crooked her fingers like quotes—" this integrity thing. And that means being open and honest, something you haven't been." She twisted around in her seat, swinging a shapely leg in the aisle. "And when he gets rid of you, I'll be right there to pick up the pieces. So, here's your warning—you tell him, or I will."

Tiffany swept out of the restaurant feeling defeated and believing that it didn't matter whether Dwayne found out from her or someone else. The bottom line was that if he knew, he would leave. She'd already put him through that never-ending divorce fiasco. When he thought Tiffany no longer had any ties to her ex, he had declared his feelings for her, only to find out that the divorce had not been totally finalized.

She might as well leave him before he left her, because it would only be a matter of time before he did.

She slid in her car, curled her hand around the photo she had taken when Chanel wasn't watching, laid her head on the steering wheel, and let the sobs take over.

CHAPTER 13

"I came to tell you to your face that I don't want nothing more to do with you." Miguel slammed his briefcase on Dwayne's desk and began unloading it. "Here's your tablet, your books, and these stupid suit jackets you made us wear." He stacked the items precariously on the edge of the desk.

Dwayne searched the face of the teen looking at him with such contempt. "What's gotten into you, Miguel?"

"The truth, that's what!"

"What in the world are you talking about?" Dwayne asked. Miguel had been one of the best scholars at Excel. And he'd never acted out. This outburst came out of left field.

Closing the briefcase, Miguel held up a wrinkled and creased newspaper clipping. "Says here you're a child molester."

He balled the paper up and threw it at Dwayne, who caught it midair.

"Was I next in line?" the angry teen asked.

"You know me better than that!" Dwayne roared, then regretted the action. The constant assassinations to his character had taken more of a toll than he realized.

"It's right here in black and white." Miguel held up his hand in mock surrender. "But let me guess. This is just 'fake news' like 'forty-five' says, right?"

"It's not news at all," Dwayne shot back, dropping the balled up paper onto the desk. "It's a bald-faced lie from people who don't want you, the other scholars or Excel to succeed."

Miguel shrugged. "I know all about that, too."

"What exactly do you think you know?" Dwayne asked, folding his arms and glaring at the boy.

"I know you're turning folks over to ICE even when they've got their papers. You're nothing but a fraud, Mr. Harper."

Dwayne steeled himself, praying for patience and inner peace. "Where are you getting this from?"

"My real father told me," Miguel shot back. "He's been coming by to see me."

Keeping his focus on Miguel for several moments, Dwayne wondered at the new development. As far as he knew, Miguel Ramos came from a home with a mother who worked to support him, his sister, and an alcoholic stepfather who contributed nothing to the household but verbal, emotional and sometimes physical abuse. Never a mention about Miguel's biological father or the possibility that he would appear. "Since when? You told me you didn't know your real father."

Miguel's gaze lowered to the carpet. "I didn't. But I do now."

"So any bozo can show up and say he's your dad, and you'll believe it?"

Miguel's finger snapped out, angled at Dwayne's chest. "Watch how you talk about my father, man."

"How do you even know for sure that this new guy, whoever he is, is your father? What's his name anyway?"

Miguel puffed his chest out. "Eduardo Sanchez."

Dwayne sank down in his executive chair, absorbing that blow. He was being hit on all sides. He had to believe that Miguel had no idea of the dirt his so-called father was involved in. Obviously, Sanchez was just using Miguel to get to Dwayne. But Dwayne knew that the teen would be too conflicted if he threw that tidbit of truth at him.

Tapping his fingers on the armrest of his executive chair, Dwayne asked, "How do you know Sanchez is telling the truth?"

"For one, we look a lot alike," Miguel said.

"That's not enough proof."

"I knew you'd say something like that. You think that because I'm a kid, I don't know anything. But I'm smarter than you think. I told him I wouldn't believe it unless we had a DNA test."

Dwayne felt his mouth drop open. "Did your mother agree to that?"

"No, I didn't tell her anything. Didn't have to," he whispered. "We got a DNA kit online."

"But that still requires your mother's consent," Dwayne countered.

Miguel averted his gaze. "Well … I put her name on the consent part because I didn't want her to know what I was doing. She kept my father from me. She's known all this time." The teen appeared to be so proud of taking matters into his own hands that Dwayne wouldn't have been surprised if he reached around and patted himself on the back. "We did the cheek swabs, sent them off to the lab, and forty-eight hours later the results were online. They told the truth."

That Sanchez was a slick one. Dwayne was familiar with the online DNA kits. He knew exactly why Sanchez chose to go that route. The results were not admissible in court because it wasn't a court-ordered legal chain of custody test.

"Miguel, you have to tell her. You can't keep this kind of secret from her."

He shook his head. "I already have enough problems."

"What kind of problems?" Dwayne asked.

"I'm working things out myself. Can't trust anybody to help me. Especially you."

"You can always trust me. I've never given you any reason to think otherwise."

"Not anymore." Miguel turned on his heels and stormed out, leaving a stunned Dwayne with a throbbing at his temples and a sadness in his heart. With each word, it was becoming obvious that he needed to get more of his brother Kings involved, especially Dro and Daron. They could get some leverage Dwayne could use against the enemy he didn't know he had made. If they failed, Dwayne wouldn't have a career, a name, or anything else left to salvage.

CHAPTER 14

"What do you mean you advise against filing the motion until a later date?" Tiffany asked her attorney.

His phone rang. He looked at the display, held up a stubby finger, and said to Tiffany, "This won't take long."

Tiffany was tired. She was frustrated. And she had no intention of spending her entire appointment waiting around while her attorney took another call. She counted to ten, then picked up her purse and stood.

Jay Barton hurried off the call. "Don't go, Tiffany. There's a lot going on in your case. I need to bring you up to speed."

"You're doggone right." She sat her purse in her lap and reclaimed the seat she had vacated. "I waited six months before even filing the divorce in the first place because you told me the law said I had to since there was no *physical* abuse during the marriage." She averted her gaze to the family photos lining the wall so he wouldn't notice the tears welling up in her eyes.

"I know," he replied, stroking the goatee on his nut-brown face. "But at that time, you said your husband just lost his job."

"Correction. He had lost *another* job. Probably the eighth one in five years."

"Well be that as it may, things were in our favor when he held a job. So I did what was best for you."

Her husband's excuse had always been the same. According to him, he was the top producer in whatever company he happened to be with at the time, but they cut him due to downsizing. She often challenged this, asking how every company he managed to get hired at suddenly downsized their staff. And why did each and every one of them get rid of their "top producer"? These divorce proceedings had always been at the mercy of Perry's laziness, greed, and selfishness.

Weariness knocked on the door of her heart. "Keeping jobs was always a problem of his during the marriage. You're telling me it's going to be an issue in the divorce too?"

"If you're the only one working, it could be." He fished a package of Tums out of his suit jacket and chomped on a couple. "He could request spousal support in the divorce decree, and with the way this particular judge tends to lean toward husbands in the cases before her, she just might give it to him."

"What?" *Tiffany shrieked. She was going to need some of those Tums if this kept up.*

"According to Illinois law, Perry can request spousal support in a divorce proceeding. And the judge would be obligated to use the State's statutory guideline to determine how much he'd be eligible to receive." *He laid a document before her.* "He could get as much as thirty-three percent of your salary since he's not working and you are."

After giving her a moment to collect herself, Jay sighed and said, "So my advice is that we wait him out. You say neither of you had savings, so he can't go too long without a job."

"He can if he finds another woman like me who's foolish enough to think it's her duty to financially support her man whenever he's out of work." Tiffany could barely contain her frustration. She crossed, then uncrossed her feet.

"Well let's hope that doesn't happen and he winds up going back to work sooner rather than later." He went through her file, licking his finger each time he turned a page. "Let's also hope that he gets a job with a salary more comparable to yours. That would take the question of spousal support off the table."

Tiffany felt her dark cloud lifting a little. "That's good to know."

The lawyer's expression changed to one she recognized from before. He wasn't done with the bad news.

"Now your 401-k is another issue," he said, his tone carrying an apology.

Tiffany felt every muscle in her body tense up. "Why?"

"Well, because all the funds in it came from monies you earned while the two of you were married, and because he has neither a 401-k nor any savings, he has the right to ask the court for a portion of your 401-k."

Tiffany almost choked on her sharp intake of breath. "Wait a minute. We already used up my 401-k from a previous job because he kept losing jobs and I was paying all the bills by myself."

She recalled being so at odds with herself when she cashed it out and held the check in her hand. A good chunk of it was taken away due to early withdrawal penalties. But what was left kept them above water for a while.

Then she started her retirement savings all over, and built it up to where it was today. And even though there were plenty times when she wanted to quit her job because it became so stressful, she did the responsible thing and stuck with it no matter how hard things became.

She stomped her foot. "And now you tell me the law will allow him to waltz away with the money I sweated blood for?"

Her attorney turned sad eyes toward her and sighed. "Sorry to say it, but yes."

"How much?"

"Could be up to half."

"Half?" Tiffany nearly slid from her seat.

Now, Perry had confessed his deception to the judge on the day he accused Tiffany of sleeping with Dwayne. Unfortunately, she had taken the bait and said. "Dwayne is an honorable man. He hasn't touched me in that way. Unlike you, he's waiting for our wedding night."

Perry's face darkened with anger as he said, "Then watch. I'm going to make sure this will take so long that he'll leave you before you ever get down the aisle."

CHAPTER 15

"Before you fight each other, you're going to have to fight me," Dwayne said, stepping between two teens standing so close to each other that their heaving chests nearly touched.

Tempers between Miguel and Kevin had been running high since classes started that morning when Miguel had mysteriously returned to Excel without any explanation whatsoever. The dissension had spilled out from their clusters and into the Chatham Boardroom, the Devon Boardroom, then found its way into the Hyde Park Boardroom.

By the time Dwayne made it there from his office, a couple teachers had separated the boys.

"I ain't got no beef with you, Mr. Harper," Kevin said, eyes never leaving Miguel's face.

"What did I tell you about using slang around me?" Dwayne demanded.

"I mean … I'm not mad at you about anything," Kevin shot back. "There's no reason for me to fight you."

"So why should I let you fight Miguel?"

"Because he says I raped his sister."

"Whoa," Dwayne said, putting a hand on Kevin's bony chest to keep him from getting hold of Miguel. He fixed his gaze on the boy's mocha face.

"I didn't rape her, Mr. Harper," Kevin protested, his hands balled into fists. "I've been going with her for two months. She didn't want him to know." He tossed a spiteful look at Miguel. "Then he caught me kissing her—"

Miguel pushed forward. The teacher behind him yanked on his shirt collar to pull him back.

The boy unbuttoned his collar, giving the stink eye to Kevin. "You were feeling all over her, treating her like a—"

"Watch what you say about her," Kevin warned, his fists in the air and poised to strike. "She's my girlfriend and she's having my baby."

"What baby?" Miguel took several steps back, almost landing spread eagle on the boardroom table.

"My sister's pregnant?! She's going to college on a scholarship in a few months and you knocked her up?"

All this teen drama was going to give Dwayne a heart attack. First, he finds out that Miguel is Eduardo's puppet and doesn't even realize it. Now Miguel's sister was pregnant. And to top it off, Tiffany had been missing in action by not returning calls or texts. He was of the mind to show up at her place unannounced, but that is never how he liked to do things. If she needed space, so be it. But he at least deserved a reason. She wouldn't even give him that. And now this.

These scholars will be the death of me. Jesus, I need you to help me. Take the wheel. Be a fence. Something.

He spoke in a quiet but authoritative tone. "You both had better figure out a way to fix this," he warned, taking in the shocked expression that Miguel still held. "And I mean right now. Young Black and Brown men are being killed everywhere for any crazy reason, and you want to add to that violence? Not going to happen. Sit down."

No one moved.

"Sit!"

They both complied.

"Now, what's this about you getting her pregnant? One of the first things we learned here was the importance of protecting your future. Everything you do today will impact your future—for good or for bad. You know that."

Kevin hung his head with shame.

"You haven't even finished school yourself. Worse than that, you don't have a way to get a decent enough job to take care of yourself, let alone a child."

"I know, I know," Kevin began, his lips trembling. "I'm sorry."

Dwayne sighed, knowing the pitfalls of parents who are ill-prepared for life's challenges. That's what had happened with him and his sister. Their mother left when they were four years old. They were blessed to have Uncle Bubba and his first wife, Rebecca, take them in. They gave Dwayne and Val a good, stable home and all the love they needed. But there was still a void because his mother had abandoned them. Issues in her life made it impossible for her to cope with the demands of a set of twins.

Thankfully, their mother came back in their lives when they were adults. He was able to forgive and forge a new relationship with her. His sister, Val, was another story.

Dwayne closed his eyes, squeezed the bridge of his nose, and then gave a pointed look to each of the boys. "We're going to get all of the parents together and talk about the best way to handle things."

Kevin and Miguel protested. Dwayne's 'don't test me' look shut their complaints up. "I'll do everything I can to help," he said. "But I'm going to need you both to do more to help yourselves. I'm going to make a call and starting tomorrow you're working at my friend's daycare. Before school. Every day. For the rest of the semester."

"Before school?" the boys protested in unison.

"Do you know how early that is?" Kevin complained.

"I sure do," Dwayne snapped. "They open at six in the morning and you'd both better have your bony butts there on time." He pointed a finger at them. "And you'd better get here on time to start class at eight."

"I don't see why I have to come," Miguel whined, folding his arms across his chest. "I'm not going to be a father."

"Keep it up," Dwayne said as he turned and walked away. "You'll be at that daycare changing diapers and wiping up spit until I retire."

"But you said you're never going to retire."

Dwayne looked over his shoulder at him. "Exactly!"

CHAPTER 16

Several fire trucks and ambulances were situated outside Miguel's grandmother's building when the Number 82 Kimball-Homan bus neared her block. He rang the bell over and over in an effort to get the driver to let him off before the designated stop. The driver paid no attention.

Almost coming to blows with his good friend Kevin two weeks ago and learning the truth about Dwayne a few weeks before that had been some of the worst things to happen in his life. That is, until he saw the drama unfolding just down the street.

The minute the driver stopped the bus and opened the door, Miguel broke out into a run and dashed in the direction of a group of people huddled together on the sidewalk, some crying, some praying, some cursing.

"That's Abuelita and her friends," Miguel whispered. His heart pumped octane through his body and he ran even faster.

He wrapped her in an embrace when he made it a few inches in front of her. "Lita," he panted. "What's happening? Are you hurt?"

She stepped back and pulled a lace hankie from her bosom to wipe the tears that fell from her eyes. "I usually say I'm fine, but I can't find it in me to say it this time, nieto."

Her eyes usually sparkled when she called him nieto, the Spanish word for grandson. But she looked listless today, as though all her fight was gone. He kissed her forehead and took hold of her elbow. "Come sit here," he said, steering her to the metal bench near the sidewalk.

"What are the fire trucks and ambulance doing here?" he asked.

She twisted around to observe the chaotic scene unfolding around them. He followed her gaze. His grandmother's neighbor, Mr. Wilbert, lay on a gurney, an oxygen mask covering most of his face. Two paramedics performed CPR. Another first responder helped Miss Norma into an ambulance transport chair and began touching a stethoscope to different parts of her chest while telling her to take deep breaths. Miss Antonia walked back and forth, wringing her hands and saying a prayer.

"The landlord put us out," Lita said. "All of us."

Miguel jumped up. "He what!?"

She pulled him back down on the bench. "Some men came here, pushing us around and throwing all our belongings outside." She pointed toward piles in the parking lot. "Our medicines. Our clothes. Our food. Our pictures. The men were arguing over who could put more of our stuff on the street. They said Caesar Wilson wanted us to know that he hated having to do this, but the building was not up to code. And that he was paying extra to the men who "helped" us get our important things out of the building. The men even sat Mr. Wilbert's safe out here. I'm sure they emptied it out first." She shook her head. "That man kept his life savings in that thing."

Miguel nodded toward two males across the street. Torn and faded jeans sagged below their hips. "Let me guess. Alonzo and Canine have been eyeballing your stuff ever since it's been put outside."

The two boys slipped into the liquor store on the corner, but kept glancing over their shoulders to take in the activity around them.

She pulled her shawl close around her. "They'll take whatever they want as soon as the fire trucks and ambulances leave."

"I won't let them do that." He gave her arms a reassuring squeeze. "Did you call the police?"

"We couldn't. Caesar's men snatched all of our house phones out the wall, and they took all our cell phones. But in spite of that, two policemen showed up out front right when Caesar's men were leaving out the back door."

Her eyebrows drew in. "It was strange though. They were asking us questions, but they acted like they weren't really interested in what was happening to us. And when we heard a fire truck siren nearby, the policemen left out of the back door really fast. They said they were going back to the station to write a report. But they never took anyone's statements or anything like that."

"Give me a minute, Lita." Miguel pulled his cell out of his pocket and dialed a number. The call went to Eduardo's voicemail. He tried again and Eduardo picked up on the second ring.

"What do you want?"

Miguel turned his back and covered his mouth to keep his grandmother from overhearing him. "Caesar Wilson put my grandmother and her friends out on the street."

"And that concerns me because …" Eduardo said in a nonchalant tone. It sounded to Miguel like the man was yawning when he said it.

Miguel pulled the phone away from his ear and looked at it, not believing his ears. "You said you would fix this," Miguel said in a muted voice.

"And I told you what it would take to make that happen. All you had to do was continue to listen to me concerning that mentor of yours," Eduardo shot back. "Instead, you let him suck you back into believing in him."

Miguel took in the chaos around him. "You insisted that I go back to Excel. I see him every day. The more I was around him, the more I saw that he wasn't the villain you said he was."

"Riiight," Eduardo drawled "Who taught you the tricks you needed to know about how to handle that Caesar Wilson? I did. I even promised to front the money for the repairs to the building. All I asked in return was for you to give me a little information on Dwayne Harper. But you punked out. Fine. You're dead to me."

The line disconnected. Miguel's heart sank to his toes. He couldn't believe that first Caesar and now Eduardo—men who should have had integrity—didn't have an ounce of it.

But there was no time to sit around and feel sorry for himself. If this situation was going to be fixed, Miguel would have to be the one to fix it.

He dialed another number. "Geo, is Dylan still with you?"

"Yeah. And you'd better not be calling to back out of the Gala work we're into. You said you'd be here as soon as you stopped by your grandmother's house."

"I've got trouble and I need your help," he said, turning to check on his grandmother. "How fast can you get here?"

"About five minutes if we take the shortcut."

"Do that. Oh, and Geo."

"Yeah."

"Come ready to beat some ass." He hung up and gave his grandmother a sheepish look. "Excuse my language, Lita."

"We all need to beat a little ass every now and then, nieto."

Miguel got up and talked to his grandmother's neighbors to find out if any of them had friends or family he could call for them. A couple had someone who could come get them. Most didn't.

He called more of his Excel classmates. Between all of these reinforcements, something would be put in place for his grandmother's friends.

CHAPTER 17

A few minutes later, Miguel found himself flanked by the two punks who'd been waiting to rummage through the senior citizens' belongings. They came as soon as the first responders left. Miguel had told his grandmother and her friends to stand back as he prepared to hold his ground against the intruders.

"You've got no reason to be here," he warned the trespassers. "This stuff belongs to someone else. Go back to where you came from."

"Man, it's finders, keepers where I come from," Alonzo said to Canine, stretching out a scarred hand to give his cronie a high-five. "I can make bank sellin' these old folks' pills." He pulled a thick stack of bills from his back pocket, licked his thumb, and started flipping through the money. Looking Miguel up and down, he asked, "They payin' you to protect them and their stuff?"

Canine cast a side glance at the ousted seniors. "Naw, these broke down old heads ain't got no money."

Tossing a one-dollar-bill at Miguel's feet, Alonzo said, "I'm payin' you to leave." He stepped close to Miguel and whispered, "*Now*, amigo. Leave now. Me and my boys got business here."

"I can't do that," Miguel said.

His grandmother called out in a voice shaking with fear, "Nieto. Maybe you'll be safer over here with us."

"Thanks, Lita. But I'm fine.

"You heard the ol' lady," Canine said, smacking a closed switchblade against his palm.

Alonzo walked past Miguel, pushing him with his shoulder. "Go somewhere and play, little boy."

Miguel turned and shoved him back. They locked arms in a bear hug. Miguel freed up a hand and landed a quick punch to Alonzo's Adam's apple. Alonzo doubled over, wheezing for breath.

Canine pulled Miguel away from his homeboy. Leering at Miguel, Canine flipped open his switchblade and jabbed at him.

Miguel jerked out of the way.

These bullies couldn't know that Excel's curriculum included martial arts and self defense.

Canine lunged again, loosing a wicked smile when his knife nicked the cuff of Miguel's shirt. The thug's eyes flicked to his companion. "You alright, man?"

Alonzo was on his hands and knees, trying to pull air into his lungs.

Miguel and Canine both glanced toward the street at the sound of multiple horns blaring. Geo and Dylan were weaving through traffic, headed in their direction, baseball bats in hand. Before they made it all the way across, a police cruiser flashed its lights and did a U-turn.

Canine returned his switchblade to his pocket and helped Alonzo up. Alonzo leaned on him as the two hobbled away.

The police car swept up to the fray. It's front passenger tire was on the curb.

Geo and Dylan flew by Miguel and the police car in pursuit of the assailants.

The officer jumped out of the cruiser. He drew his weapon and aimed at the boys, taking care to keep his body shielded behind the car door. "Halt! Police!"

Miguel put his hands up and slowly turned his head toward Geo and Dylan, who stopped running.

"All three of ya, on the ground now!" the pasty-skinned officer demanded.

Miguel dropped to his knees.

"Officer," Miguel's grandmother pleaded. "He's—"

"Not now, ma'am." He spoke a few words into his shoulder mic.

The only word Miguel could make out was "backup."

The officer advanced toward them, still training his gun on them. "You two," he said to Geo and Dylan. "Hands behind your heads."

The boys raised their arms cautiously, lacing their fingers behind their necks.

"Now walk backward toward me."

They took several small steps back. When they were inches away from Miguel, the policeman said, "On your knees."

They knelt beside Miguel. The officer holstered his weapon and secured zip ties on their wrists.

"Sir," Miguel's grandmother began.

"In a minute, ma'am," he snapped, agitation brimming in his tone. Turning his attention to the teens, he said, "What are your names?"

"Miguel Ramos, sir."

"Giovani Russo, sir."

"Dylan Alexander Wright, Junior, sir."

"And just what were you doing here?" he demanded. "Because somebody up the street called 911 and said that some hoodlums stole a bunch of property from the folks in this building and were selling it on the street." His eyes swept over the scene. "And from the looks of things, that's just what happened."

He squinted at Dylan. "You with the surgical mask on your face. You must be the ringleader."

"No, sir," Dylan responded. "I have really bad allergies, and the weatherman said there's a lot of mold and pollen in the air today. So I have to wear a mask to keep from triggering my allergies."

"I might have believed you, boy, except that you're wearing this hoodie, your heads all covered up, and it's a good ninety degrees out here. And who needs such dark sunglasses on a cloudy day like today?" He fingered the thick material of Dylan's hoodie. "Yeah, you look like some thief trying to hide his identity."

"Sir, no, sir," Dylan responded. "I have to protect my skin and eyes from the sun at all times because I'm albino."

"Albino my ass. You're nothing more than a high yellow—"

"Sir," Miguel cut in. "He's telling you the truth. Look at his skin and hair. They don't have any color. And his eyes are red instead of brown."

Dylan flinched when the policeman snatched off his hood. He lowered his head so the sun's rays wouldn't hit him so hard.

"I've seen plenty of you people wearing this bleached blonde hair." He grabbed hold of Dylan's jaw and forced his head up. "And your eyes are probably red from smoking that dope."

Dylan snatched his head away.

"And what does that 'NOAH' on your sweatshirt stand for? If I had to guess, I'd say … um … Network … Of … American … Hoodlums." He was the only one who chuckled.

Geo spoke up for his friend. "It stands for National Organization for Albinism and Hypopigmentation."

"Hypo what?"

"Hypopigmentation," Dylan said with malice now lacing his words. "That means not enough color in the skin. Albino. Can you get that through your—"

Miguel redirected the discussion before his friend's mouth landed all three of them in jail. "My grandmother is right over there with the others. We're here to help them, not rob or hurt them. They got evicted illegally, and we were keeping some other guys from messing with them and their stuff. And we're going to have to help them find somewhere to live."

"Young man," Miguel's grandmother said to the officer from a distance. "Please, may I talk to you?" She inched closer.

The officer glared at each of the boys. "I guess we're about to get to the bottom of this now. Any confessions you boys want to make before this nice lady tells me what really happened?"

"No, sir," they said in unison.

He beckoned for Miguel's grandmother to come even closer, then escorted her to the cruiser. He opened the back door and helped her in, then listened as she talked.

When she finished, he removed his hat, scratched his head, and turned to look at the teens. Deep furrows made indentations between his brows as he spoke into his shoulder mic again.

He looked up into the midday sun. Tiny rivulets of sweat dripped down his temple. He wiped them away and said, "Well, boys. This must be your lucky day." He tossed his head toward Miguel's grandmother. "Lady here says you're telling the truth. She was too far away from us to hear the story you told me. But it matches what she said, so I'll take her word." He cut off their zip ties. "Just stay out of trouble."

"My troubles didn't start until you rolled up and handcuffed us for no reason," Miguel muttered.

"What was that, boy?"

"I was just saying that we're going to start making some phone calls, sir, so the tenants won't be left homeless," he amended. "You think you can help with that. I mean, now that you know the truth and all."

The policeman slicked his hair back and put his hat back on his head before returning to the police car and leaving the scene.

Miguel watched the cruiser tear down the street. "Just like I thought."

Geo breathed a sigh of relief. "Maybe we should call Mr. Harper."

"No, he already has enough to handle," Miguel said. "We need to do this on our own."

The boys started making calls. They received a few call-backs from the churches they reached out to. One church even called a news crew to come out and cover the story.

Miguel, Geo and Dylan would not leave until they had secured temporary accommodations for each of the seniors.

"That's what Mr. Harper taught us to do," Miguel said hours later when they were done.

CHAPTER 18

"You can die for all I care," Eduardo Sanchez snarled.

Those words and Eduardo Sanchez's hate-filled face were things that would never leave Miguel's mind.

Hands raised, Eduardo took small backward steps until he found himself pressed against the east gate of the Excel campus. Except for the twitching of his downturned mouth and the gnashing of his teeth, he held his body stiff and shot a menacing stare at the gun pointed at him.

Miguel felt the muscles in his hand twitch as he gripped a revolver trained in Eduardo's direction. The man's groin was the bullseye. His stepfather's gun would finally serve the purpose it should—putting a coward out of his misery.

"You just had to do it, right?" Miguel snarled. "It wasn't enough to hurt me by hurting my grandmother and her friends? You could have gone to your grave without telling me the things you said on that voicemail," the teen yelled.

Out the corner of his eye, Miguel could see a body slowly approaching. Sean Murray, one of Excel's martial arts instructors, came into view. He made sure to keep his hands visible as he inched closer and called out to the boy.

Miguel didn't blink an eye.

"Nobody's going to hurt you, son," Sean said. "Just give me the gun." He gingerly extended a hand toward Miguel.

Dwayne rounded the corner and skidded to a stop. "Miguel, do what the man says," he instructed a reassuring tone.

The boy lifted the weapon to Eduardo's temple before meeting Dwayne's gaze.

"You don't want to do this, Miguel." Dwayne took one step closer to him with each word.

Eduardo quietly sidestepped further away from the action.

Miguel's hand trembled, not from the weight of the gun but from the weight of the emotional boulder he carried on his shoulder. "I went to him for help," he said, moving the gun around like it was a laser pointer used during a presentation. "He made everything worse. He's the reason my Abuelita was put out on the street."

All three men crouched to avoid been accidentally shot while Miguel waved the gun around with each angry word.

The boy let his head drop to his chest. A pair of strong arms surrounded him before he hit the ground.

Prodding the gun away from him, Dwayne said, "You can't let him get in your head, Miguel. You're working too hard to be something. Don't let him be the reason you throw it all away." He handed the weapon to the security guard, who aimed it at Eduardo.

"He said if I didn't help him destroy you, he would hurt someone I loved." He looked at Dwayne with sad eyes. "Mr. Harper, I'm sorry for the accusations I made. I know better now."

Dwayne clasped Miguel's shoulder. "That's water under the bridge. Don't fret yourself over it. We're cool, okay?" he said, extending his hand for a fist bump. "And what's this about your grandmother being put on the street?"

"He promised to help me fight her slumlord, but he wouldn't do it because I wouldn't turn against you."

"That's lowdown and foul, but it's not enough to make you put a gun to your head or to want to shoot someone else. Boy, you could have ruined your whole future. And over what?" He glared at him. "A worthless human who would use a child in his game to discredit me? He is so not worth it."

Miguel took out his phone, put it on speaker, played a voicemail. "He left this message for me today," he said, tossing an angry look at Eduardo.

"He said if I didn't help him destroy you, he would hurt someone I loved."

Eduardo's voice was loud and clear as he detailed how he had sexually assaulted Miguel's mother before he was born—and what a whore she was. And how worthless Miguel was because he was never wanted by his mother and certainly not by his father.

Eduardo bared his teeth. "You'd better get bail money ready, Harper, because I'm going straight to the police." He reached for his jacket pocket, but thought better of it when the security guard cocked the trigger of the pistol. "Nobody pulls a gun on me. Not you," he said to Sean. "And certainly not him," he said, looking at Miguel with the flames of hell burning in his eyes. "I'll make that crack baby spend the rest of his life in prison."

Dwayne let out a slow hum. "Sanchez, I advise you to keep your mouth shut or I'll shoot you up my damn self. I have every reason to." He made a call, keeping his gaze on Eduardo. When he hung up, he told Miguel, "Dro, Jai and Daron will be here shortly to help sort this all out. Hiram's on his way. I want you to talk with him."

"Why?" Miguel asked.

"Because I need you to hear from him how trading your life for one behind bars is not the answer." Dwayne pinned a glare on Eduardo.

"And everything that happened here today stays here, or so help me, I'm going to let my brothers loose on you and you'll wish you were dead when they're done. Understand?"

Eduardo swallowed hard but agreed.

CHAPTER 19

"Is the team going to be any good this year?" Dwayne asked Uncle Bubba as they gathered the bats, gloves and balls that Dwayne and his brother Kings had donated to a team put together by Dwayne's church. With all the upheaval in his life these past few months, sitting in the park on a spring day was a welcome relief for Dwayne. Plus, the Kings and the Knights were coming to support.

"You tell me about the team. See Chad over there?" Uncle Bubba pointed to a five-year-old who was racing toward the home plate. Head back, chest high, arms pumping, Chad hit the ground near home base, then slid in feet first.

"That boy hit the ball and took off runnin'," Uncle Bubba said. "But the first baseman caught it and tagged him out. 'Cept Chad never stopped runnin'. The boy at first threw the ball to second, and Chad got tagged out there. Same thing happened at third base, but he kept runnin'. I ain't never seen one man get tagged out four times off one hit."

The men shared a hearty laugh. When the team had been formed, the players were allowed to vote on what it would be named. "Crushers" was their choice, because they were going to squash all the other teams. With players like Chad, that remained to be seen.

Dwayne glanced at his phone, noticing he had not received a call or text from Tiffany. Lately, she'd distanced herself and he still didn't understand why. He'd sent breakfast from Batter & Berries, and lunch from Mabel's, a Jamaican restaurant that Shaz highly recommended, to her floor in the hospital wing where she worked. And he'd also sent flowers and a massage therapist to her home. If she didn't want to lay eyes on him, he could at least show that he cared.

"Uncle Bubba, how did you know Miss Greta was the woman for you?"

His gaze shifted from the hilarious play of the game in front of them to Dwayne. "The first day I saw Greta, I knew she was gonna be my wife."

"And what did she have to say about that?" Dwayne asked as he folded their lawn chairs.

"Well, I didn't tell her for a whole year."

Dwayne tipped the cooler to the side to let the melted ice run out. "Why? Frightened that she was going to shoot you down?" He removed the juice boxes and put them on the bench so the boys could each grab one when the coach finished giving them their end-of-game pep talk.

"No, that wasn't it," his Uncle said, reaching down to pick up a candy bar wrapper off the ground and put it in the nearby trash receptacle. "It's just that I needed God to work on my heart."

"Unc, you're one of the best men I know. Shoot, I try to be like you. You're good-hearted and you genuinely care about people." He opened a Frito Lays variety pack and put it beside the juice boxes. "What needed fixing?"

"It's one thing to love family and friends," Uncle Bubba said, swiping one of the juices. "It's a whole other thing to love a woman the way she deserves to be loved." He poked a straw through the top of the juice box. "After I lost your Aunt Rebecca, I thought I'd never love again. All that changed when I met Greta. We joke and say it's an "arranged marriage" because God brought us together. But she deserved to have the best of my love, not some leftovers from a broken heart."

Dwayne absorbed that for a moment, reflecting on his confusing relationship with Tiffany. He had been a friend—a good one, he might add. He'd also been patient through everything, and only when the ink was about to dry on that paperwork, only when he knew she was about to be free of a man who only sought to drain her dry, did he share that his feelings had slowly transformed into love. Only then.

"Speaking of love," Dwayne said, slipping a Crushers baseball cap on his head. "I … well, I uh … I sorta have a little dilemma."

"Spit it out, boy," Uncle Bubba said. He took a deep swig from the juice box. "What is it?"

"It's Tiffany. She keeps pulling further and further away. And this divorce thing seems like it's never going to end. That man is spiteful and petty."

His uncle's head snapped around to focus on Dwayne. "It's not her fault her ex is dragging this out. He doesn't want to let her go. He's punishing her because she dared to leave him and fall in love with you."

But the day that the judge was all set to put an end to the abusive and manipulative marriage—which Tiffany admitted had been on a downward spiral from the time they said "I do"—Perry pulled a fast one. Out of spite, he had his lawyer come before the judge to confess that Perry had withheld information about money he hid. The lawyer submitted a motion requesting that Perry be given time to gather and submit his new financial info to the court and to Tiffany's attorney.

Translation: an unexpected and deeply troubling delay that came into play just when Tiffany thought she'd made it to the end of the process and freedom was within her grasp. All because Perry suddenly found a "conscience" and wanted to come clean.

"I'm beginning to wonder if she doesn't want to let go of that ex of hers," Dwayne said as Uncle Bubba smashed the empty juice box and tossed it in the trash receptacle. "I mean, it's like the more I love her, the more she distances herself. And she seems to think I want to be with Chanel."

Uncle Bubba's eyebrows shot up, his gaze narrowed to slits. "Who's Chanel? I know you better not be messin' around on Tiffany. I taught you better than that."

"I'm not interested in Chanel Bordeaux, Unc. She's just someone who might be able to help me iron out a few problems concerning the school. That's all. She put an offer on the table, but I haven't taken her up on it because I don't trust her. But I'm also careful because I don't want to create another enemy either."

"Does Tiffany know this?"

"Yes, I explained it all to her. But between that and what's happening with her ex-husband, she's moving further and further away from me emotionally."

Uncle Bubba put his eyes on the game and chuckled when a player slid, but totally missed home plate and took out the player who was standing there. "Sounds like you've been really patient, nephew. But I had to do the same thing with your Aunt Greta. I knew that before I approached her, I had to work some things out in my heart so I could love her right. But I didn't prepare myself for her to need time too. She had promised herself that she wouldn't marry again. Her heart had been broken into too many pieces, and once she healed from it, she wasn't about to put it out there to get hurt again. I had to spend time showing her that she could trust her heart to me."

"I hear what you're saying, Unc," Dwayne said, grimacing when the next player swung and the bat flew out of his hand.

"Then woo Tiffany. Wait for her. Support her. She's dealing with a lot. But she'll come around. You just keep lovin' on her. It'll work out." He clapped his nephew on the back as the Kings and the Knights arrived and fanned out around them.

"How much did we raise?" Hiram asked Dwayne.

"Not as much as I'd like." Dwayne put his focus on the rest of the men who leaned in for their "men" hugs.

"How about a friendly wager?" Hiram said to the Kings and the Knights.

"How so?" Reno asked, rolling up his sleeves.

"Knights against the Kings. Losers make up the difference for what Dwayne didn't raise today."

The Kings shared a glance among them as the Knights moved so they were grouped together.

"Nah, you youngsters can't handle us."

Falcon playfully sniffed the air and said, "I smell ... Popeye's chicken." Three of the Knights started clucking, causing everyone to laugh.

"More like Kentucky Fried," Hiram taunted.

"What do you say, brothers?" Dwayne said to his fellow Kings. "Let's show them what we're made of."

"Oh no, see," Hiram said, smiling. "I think it's the Knights who's going to show you all how it's done."

Folks stayed to watch the exciting game between the two groups of men, who kept the crowd in stitches with their trash-talk and antics. In the end, the game was to be continued as a torrential rain came down right at the point that they were tied. So, all of them chipped in to make up Dwayne's deficit, but the challenge was on the table for them to come back out and finish what they started.

CHAPTER 20

"Do you know how much it hurts me when you treat me like I've hurt you or like I'm going to hurt you?" Dwayne asked Tiffany.

She cringed at his accusatory tone. She'd been dodging his calls, ignoring his texts, and breaking dates with him. Somehow, after a conversation with Temple, Autumn and Zuri, she found the courage to show up at his house for tonight's dinner date. It was the sixth invitation he had sent. He refused to simply show up uninvited and unannounced at her house.

Riley, the neighbor's cat, moseyed over in Dwayne's backyard and rubbed himself against the leg of the glider Dwayne and Tiffany sat in. Dwayne shooed him away. Riley turned up his nose, but left.

Dwayne gathered Tiffany's hands in his. "I'm glad you're here. I really am. Because I really want to understand why you're pushing me away from you."

At least his voice didn't sound as demanding as it had a minute ago.

"Then you turn around and accuse me of wanting to be with Chanel," he said. "And this comes after you took a meeting with her in my place. I thought for sure she would lay out her plans for helping with the school and put any concerns you had to rest."

Tiffany looked down and picked at the floral pattern cushion on the glider.

"You know I'm not a cheating man, Tiff. If I wanted Chanel, I would've told you that you were not the one for me."

She couldn't find the right words to say. Her shoulders dropped and she bit her lip.

Dwayne softened his tone even more. "I want you. Just you." He pushed a foot against the ground, sending the glider in a gentle forward and backward motion. "But it feels like you don't want me anymore; don't want us anymore. And for the life of me, I don't understand what's happening and why. I can't begin to address a problem when I don't know what the problem is."

She exhaled loudly, then wiped her hands on her tailored copper slacks. "I've been hiding something from you for a long time. And there's something about Chanel's presence that forces me to deal with it—whether I'm ready or not."

The silence between them was damning.

"Do you trust me?" he asked, following her when she stood and moved away. He turned her to face him so his eyes were pinned to hers.

She nodded, but the move was slow in coming.

"Well, tell me what it is so we can work through it together." He caressed her hand, which had a slight tremor. "I hate to see you hurting like this."

"I had a child when I was fourteen years old," she blurted, then put distance between them. She shrank away at the touch of his hand on her wrist.

"Tiffany, don't shut me out," he pleaded, placing a hand on her waist. She settled her nerves enough to allow him to guide her back to the glider.

"Why did you keep this from me for so long?" he asked.

"I was too ashamed." She wrapped her arms around her midsection and slowly rocked back and forth.

"My parents were trying to cozy up to people who they thought could further their political careers," she said just barely above a whisper. "They wanted everyone to think they had the perfect family. They kept such a tight reign on me. More like a noose."

Her rocking was replaced with the wringing of her hands. "I couldn't hang out with any kids from school or even the kids on the block because my parents felt they were beneath us. I basically went to school and church. No movies. No going to the mall with a group of girls. Then one day, Damien Jackson moved to our block."

"I don't think I ever heard you mention his name," Dwayne noted. "A schoolgirl crush?"

She nodded. "More than a crush. All the girls wanted him. I was fourteen and about to go into my freshman year of high school." She felt foolish opening herself up like this, but she pressed on. "That boy sure did sweet-talk me. He told me how pretty I was. No one ever told me I was pretty. Said he liked me more than the other girls because I was smart and because I understood a solitary guy like him."

Dwayne looked at her with such sympathy, like he was wondering how many teardrops had bathed her long lashes.

"I was so naïve," Tiffany whispered, her voice breaking with emotion. "I nearly jumped out of my skin when he tried to kiss me one day on my screened-in porch. But those sweet words kept coming, and one kiss on the first day turned into heavy petting within a month. Next thing you know, I was missing my period."

She gave a weak smile that didn't quite reach her eyes. "When I told him I was pregnant, he shut me completely out. Even demanded that the teacher switch assignment partners because I would be too distracting to work with."

Tiffany had cried nonstop that day. She walked around in a daze for the longest time, but her parents didn't see her distress. But when a few months passed and she started picking up weight in all the tell-tale places, her parents flipped out. They snatched her out of school and sent her to live with a distant cousin in Alabama until the baby was born.

Dwayne blanched as her story went on. But she had already opened the coffin containing this dead secret. Couldn't re-bury it. Might as well do a full autopsy on her past.

"My parents knew their secret was safe with that woman—her name was Linda Bryers—because she had wanted a baby and they were going to give her mine. It wasn't even a real adoption. And Miss Linda actually walked around telling folks she was pregnant."

Linda was a great seamstress, and she sewed a belly-shaped pillow to strap around her waist under her clothes. All day, every day, she wore that thing, adding a little more stuffing to it each week to make it look like her pregnancy was progressing. No one questioned anything.

Tiffany had known what was going on. But she was unable to turn to anyone for help because Miss Linda lived in the middle of nowhere.

"When my time came, I gave birth right there in her bathroom." Tiffany's eyes glazed with tears as Dwayne tightened his hold on her hands. "Miss Linda padded the tub with quilts and made me stay there until I delivered. Said it would be easier for her to clean up afterward."

The woman could afford to throw them away because Tiffany's mother had paid a bankroll to cover up their secret.

"My mother was already there because they agreed that she'd come down in my eighth month and stay until the baby was born, then take me back to Chicago right afterward. So she came from the hotel to watch her grandchild being born. Then she allowed Miss Linda to name her, clean her, love her, and raise her as her own." She put her eyes on Dwayne, whose expression was so filled with compassion that her heart swelled with love. "That's why I felt so jealous when Chanel came on the scene," Tiffany confessed. "She could offer you more than I ever could. She's a professional and could help you with what you love to do most—educate. She seemed to love children, and they loved her back. I had a child that I was forced to give away by parents who didn't know what love was. That made me feel more insecure than you can know."

Dwayne held onto Tiffany as the tears came and turned into full sobs. "And you're wrong," he whispered. "What I love most … is you, Tiffany. I don't know how many ways that I can say that." He stroked a finger across her face. "One thing Khalil encouraged us to have is a passion that fulfills us. A purpose. And there is no greater purpose than loving a woman who doesn't know how much she deserves to be loved."

Tiffany cried into the wall of his chest. His muscular arms wrapped about her as he kissed her forehead and expressed his love for her. How could she ever doubt this man? His love had always felt true.

She ran her finger along his tattoos. A lion's face was in the center of three circles on the underside of each wrist. The mane looked like flames. Nine spearheads were situated between the bottom of the two circle. It was a nod to the nine Kings of the Castle, Dwayne's brothers-in-arms.

When her crying ceased, he kissed her tenderly and asked, "Where is your daughter now?"

"I don't know," she answered, wiping her tears with the back of a trembling hand. "When I turned eighteen, I started looking for Miss Linda. I Googled everything I remembered about her. Her name. Her address. I couldn't find any trace of her. I did connect with the people who moved in the house after her."

Tiffany squeezed her eyes shut as the horrific memories zipped through her mind, ones that had been the source of nightmares when she believed all manner of evil could have been visited on her child.

"They didn't know where Miss Linda went. But worse than that, they said that when she showed them the house before they bought it, it was fully furnished but there was no baby nor was there any type of baby stuff in any of the rooms. She showed them every room. They opened every closet and cabinet because they needed plenty of storage space. No crib. No bottles. No stroller. No baby."

She gripped Dwayne's hand. "I fell apart. Did my baby die? Did she sell him? Did she give him away? Whatever happened to him, it was my fault because I wasn't there to protect him."

There was a silence as they both processed the grief that had been laid out before them.

"Tiffany, you were only fourteen years old. You couldn't protect yourself, much less a newborn. You have to let that guilt go, baby. It's killing you. It's killing us. I don't think any less of you now that I know this. It makes me love you even more and want to keep you safe. Even if you couldn't talk to me about it, why didn't you at least tell Val? She would have helped you process it."

"I was afraid she'd tell you," Tiffany said. "I mean, you're her twin brother. Why wouldn't she want to keep you from trying to make a life with the wrong woman?"

He tilted his head and peered at her. "Now you know her better than that. You're her friend, but does she talk to you about the people she's helping?"

"Never."

"Well, she wouldn't tell anyone your business either. Not even me," he admitted, wiping the last remnants of tears from under her chin. "Dry your tears and don't even think about Chanel. You never have to worry about her. She is a non-issue."

Somehow, he didn't sound as sure as Tiffany would have liked.

CHAPTER 21

Eduardo took a few quick strides to fall in step behind Chanel when she stepped out of Bloomingdale's. He tipped up to her, pulled her coat tail, and said, "Guess who?"

Chanel shrieked, dropping her bag. Clutching several others to her chest, she turned to face her attacker. When her eyes latched onto Eduardo, her frightened look gave way to shock.

"Not happy to see me?" he asked, picking her things up.

"You know you didn't have to do that," she chided. The bags hanging from her wrist rustled against each other as she took the Bloomingdale's bag from him.

"If you'd answer my calls, I wouldn't have to stalk you."

Chanel Bordeaux was an intelligent woman who had worked her way up the Commission's ranks and had became a valuable asset to any organization she aligned herself with. But she also had a predictable weakness. She spent every Saturday pampering and spoiling herself on Chicago's Magnificent Mile—with Eduardo's money. After a massage, a facial, and a mani-pedi at Mario Tricoci's Day Spa, she would spread his wealth at Bloomingdale's, Gucci, Michael Kors and Kate Spade.

"I'll call you as soon as I finish shopping," she said, stepping around him.

He pulled her arm, snatching her out of the path of an old woman on a motorized wheelchair who seemed to be intent on mowing down half the shoppers in sight.

"I just saved your life," he whispered to her. "The least you can do is sit a few minutes and talk to me." He nodded toward a less populated area. When she didn't move, he gave an exaggerated pout.

Chanel huffed loudly and led the way through the shoppers to take a seat on a bench facing the cosmetics counter.

Eduardo followed, choosing to stand instead of taking the space beside her. When he weaved his fingers through the curly hair spilling onto her shoulder, she moved her head away.

It took all of his willpower to keep from yanking her head back and wrapping his fingers around her throat. He knew she was aware that side of him existed. She'd just been smart enough to not be on the receiving end of it up until this point. But she just might, if he didn't like the answers he got from her.

Looking down his nose at Chanel, he asked, "So why haven't you reported back to let me know how things are going with Harper?"

She laid her bags on the space next to her, putting a little more distance between them. "Report back? You make it seem like I'm merely someone who works for you. I'm your woman—at least, that's what I thought I was."

"Funny, I thought the same thing. But then you started avoiding me. All my calls go to your voicemail. And to make matters worse, you don't even give me the courtesy of returning them."

She opened her mouth to protest, but swallowed her words when Farrell's song Happy sounded off from the phone in her purse.

"Answer it," Eduardo said.

"It can wait," she replied, shrugging it off

"Well, it must be somebody special." He narrowed his gaze on her.

"They were important enough that you gave them their own ringtone. Guess I didn't measure up."

When the song stopped, he took out his phone and dialed her number. Her phone remained silent. Ending the call and slipping his phone back into his coat pocket, Eduardo said, "Did you block me?"

A wave of crimson traveled up Chanel's face. She rubbed the back of her neck. "What did you want to talk to me about?"

He squatted in front of her, placing a hand on her knee. "Giving me that tidbit about Dwayne Harper at the parenting class was good and all." He ran a finger along her slender ankle. "But surely you've uncovered more dirt than that in all this time."

Chanel gave a haughty lift of her head. "Not really. He lives a pretty clean-cut life."

He stood to his full height. "Don't act like you don't know how this works. If there's no dirt, create some." He pointed to her purse and snapped his fingers. "Until you have what I need, my credit cards please."

Her eyes widened at first, then her shoulders drooped with defeat. She opened the purse and shoved a hand in it. "Here," she said, pulling out the wallet and smacking an American Express and Discover card in his open palm.

"If we have to have this talk again, I won't take something away from you. I'll give something to you." He opened her hand, placed a bullet in it, and closed her hand around it.

Beads of sweat formed above her upper lip as all color drained from her skin.

He walked off, leaving her to digest his words.

CHAPTER 22

"The Gala is two weeks away and you're telling me you're too far behind on the preparations to make your part of the event happen?"

Dwayne eyed each student in the Evanston Boardroom one by one. Most of them hung their head. The rest couldn't meet his eyes.

"Excel's reputation is on the line, not to mention your grades." He paced in front of the desk. "You know we don't have any room for error. The State is just looking for a reason to permanently shut us down. And with this Gala being part of the curriculum, and so visible to everyone in the community, it can make or break us."

He was sorely disappointed that the same scholars who had been stellar when it came to their assignments, had somehow let this most important one fall apart.

Miguel raised his hand. "Mr. Harper, sir." He swallowed hard under Dwayne's glare. "We … um … we fell behind because we were working on something more important."

Dwayne looked at him as though he'd lost his mind. He was well aware of every assignment and every project that the cluster of scholars were involved in. "What can be more important than keeping this school open?" He massaged his temples then raised his hands in surrender. "Never mind."

Everything Dwayne had gone through was to benefit the kids and give them a future. Quitting wasn't in his nature. He'd found the resolve and perseverance to stand against every attack launched against him. But he was at a point where he didn't have it in him to fight a battle the kids obviously didn't want him to win. He put his head in his hands, trying to wrap his mind around these new developments. This team, more than the others, excelled at their studies.

Miguel stood and beckoned for Geo and Dylan to join him at the front of the class. The other six stayed at the table. "Mr. Harper," he said timidly.

Dwayne let his hands slide down his face. "What is it, Miguel?"

"Well, sir, the reason the Gala's not totally done according to our original projections and timeline is because we've been spending all our time looking for housing for my grandmother and all the people who live in her building."

"But when you told me about them being put out of their apartments, you said the churches you contacted had found places for them to stay."

"They did, Mr. Harper," Geo replied.

"But it was just temporary," Dylan added.

Dwayne dropped down into the nearest seat, gesturing for them to explain.

The whole group joined in to tell the story of how they were still working together to get permanent residences for the evicted seniors and justice from Caesar Wilson.

"And you've been doing this all by yourselves?" Dwayne asked, a sense of pride rising up in him.

They all nodded eagerly.

"And you didn't think to come to me for help?" Dwayne chided.

"Come on, Mr. Harp," Miguel said. "You showed us how important it is to have a humanitarian heart. And the things we're learning here are giving us the tools to create, implement, and execute a plan."

Several students balled up pieces of paper and threw them at him. "Man, do you always have to throw in all those words you see on Wikipedia?" Geo joked.

"These are words we learned in class," he shot back. "If I went to the trouble of memorizing them, I might as well use them every now and then. Besides, I can't help it if the rest of you are satisfied with having the vocabulary of a third-grader," Miguel taunted, laughing as he ducked more paper bombs coming his way.

"Okay, okay," Dwayne said with a broad smile on his face. "Break it up." He motioned for Miguel, Geo, and Dylan to take their seats. "I have to say, knowing all the details, I'm more proud than you could imagine."

"We don't want to let you down, Mr. Harper," Dylan said from the back of the room.

"And I won't let you down," Dwayne replied.

"We'll work twice as hard to bring our part of the Gala up to speed this week," Geo said.

Dwayne shook his head. "What you're doing with the seniors is more important than the Gala because peoples' lives are at stake." He scanned the expectant faces of his scholars and formulated a new plan. "I'm going to call in reinforcements to help you get both the Gala and the relocation project to the finish line."

CHAPTER 23

"This is fifty thousand dollars!"

Tiffany ran a finger across the cashier's check, counting the zeroes to confirm that her eyes had seen the correct amount. This money was more than everything in her modest condo cost.

"I told you I was going to pay off your debt, didn't I?" Dwayne extracted the check from her and laid it on the coffee table, then wrapped his arms around Tiffany's waist. "You didn't believe I was going to do it?"

She inhaled slowly, taking in a calming breath. "It's not that at all. I know you are a man of integrity. In the three years that I've known you, you always do whatever you say you're going to do."

Dwayne placed his hand in the small of her back and guided her to the couch. They sank into the soft leather cushions. Lifting her chin and examining her face, Dwayne said, "You seem … sad. What's wrong, baby?"

Tiffany felt tears welling up in her eyes. When she looked down, Dwayne got on his knees in front of her and looked up into her face.

"Why are you crying, baby? I thought this would make you happy." He wiped away the tears that had fallen down her cheek. "You were so worried you would have to file bankruptcy because you're responsible for the marriage debt, even though you weren't the one who incurred that debt."

"It does make me happy," she whispered. "I just didn't expect that you'd do this until *after* we were married."

"I get it," he said with a smile, his voice a soothing balm to her unsettled nerves. "You think that since I haven't been able to pin you down to set a date, this money is supposed to be an incentive to guilt you into marrying me."

Rising, Dwayne extended his hand and helped Tiffany stand. "When I said I was going to pay off your debt, it wasn't based on us getting married. I love you. I love your heart. I love the person you are. And knowing all the things you endured during your previous marriage, I just want to do all I can to be the man that helps restore everything you lost. The finances you lost. The emotional security you lost. The respect you lost. The self-love you lost. The ability to receive love."

He pressed a kiss to her cheek. "Tiffany, all I want is to help make you whole again. When you walk into the courthouse today, I don't want you to be bound by any financial debt tied to him. I don't want that to be any consideration."

She laid her forehead on his broad chest.

"I hate you went through what you went through," he whispered, wrapping his arms around her. "But you survived, baby. You fought to regain your life. And you're winning. Every day that I see that smile, you're winning. Every day that I see you reaching out to others in love, you're winning. And every day that I get to be loved by you, we're winning."

Tiffany pressed her body against him. He brushed his lips against her temple, then they shared a tender kiss.

She pulled away, gently touched the tip of his nose. "You are amazing and I'm thankful to God that He brought you to me."

"Sometimes He puts a point in the win column," Dwayne said with a wink.

* * *

"Your Honor," Tiffany's attorney, Jay Barton, began. "Can we put an end to these proceedings with my client's motion to forgo all support or any offers of money on Mr. Richards' behalf? He's been stalling and drawing this out by finally admitting that he lied to this court and then taking nearly half a year to bring in all of the assets he's had hidden away throughout the entire marriage. Most of it amounts to everything my client put into their finances to keep them afloat."

He put a glare on Perry, who raised his chin in a haughty gesture that made him seem more like a toddler than a grown man. "My client wants nothing more than her freedom. And unlike Tina Turner, she doesn't even want to keep his last name."

A few chuckles from the bailiff and the court reporter came behind that one. The judge put an eye on them and shut it down.

"Well, Mr. Richards, what do you have to say for yourself?"

"Your Honor, I just want to do what's right and fair, that's all." Perry shrugged. "It's taken me a minute to find all the documents. I want to show you that I'm an honest man. That's only fair, right?"

"Honestly, Jay," Tiffany whispered to her attorney, who had to place a hand over his mouth to hold in a laugh.

"And then there's the house." Perry rocked on his heels. "It's her house. My name is only on the deed, but she should sell it and split the money."

"Actually," Judge Breedlaw said. "You've had ample time to sell the place, and you're the one who's benefitted because you live there." She sighed before putting a focus on Tiffany and her counsel, then on Perry, who scowled at the admonishment. "I'm ready to finally put this divorce to rest."

"But wait—"

"Wait, what?" Judge Breedlaw snapped. "You lied to this court. Then carried out a year-long delay-of-game to stop the inevitable from happening. It's over."

Perry dropped down into his chair, shrugging off his attorney's attempts at keeping him calm.

"The house. Ms. Richards, how do you want to handle it?" the judge asked. "Did you still want to try to sell it yourself?"

Tiffany looked at Dwayne, who shook his head. "No, Your Honor. My ex-husband is still there and I believe he'll sabotage any efforts made in that direction. Like he's already done in the past."

"So what would you like to do?"

"Give it back to the bank in a Deed in Lieu of Foreclosure."

"What?!" Perry was on his feet.

"Mr. Richards, you need to plant your butt in that seat and be quiet. It's been the Perry Richards show for the last three years. It's time that Tiffany Richards took the stage before I draw the final curtain."

"But that would destroy my good credit," he complained.

"Actually, only her credit would be taking the hit because your name is just on the deed, not the mortgage note," the judge noted.

He huffed.

"Besides, you only have good credit because I paid the bills," Tiffany shot back. "Grow a pair and pay your own."

The bailiff gave a low whistle. Dwayne blinked twice, then fixed his mouth so a chuckle wouldn't escape. He nodded, then did a quick jab with his fist, signaling an air "fist bump".

"But I thought you were so concerned about your good credit," Perry goaded.

"With what I'm about to do with my life," Tiffany countered. "I won't have to worry about it. I'll recover from whatever you've done to me financially, just like I've overcome what you've done to me physically, mentally, and emotionally."

The judge's smirk was not hard to miss. "On that note, I'll issue my final decree. All of the assets that were accumulated throughout the marriage will be split between you. All of the assets that were submitted to this court *after* Mr. Richards wasted the court's time will go to the Petitioner in its entirety."

Perry jumped to his feet. The judge favored him with a glance. The attorney yanked him back down into the chair.

"That should be enough to cover whatever the bank will say is owing on the house and you can clear your name credit-wise," the judge said. "As of today, this will be the final decree and I'd like all of the signatures to be done before everyone walks out of here."

"You can't do that," Perry said, taking a step toward the judge's bench.

The bailiff jumped in front of him like a barricade.

"Really?" the judge said. "Sign the decree, Mr. Richards."

"Or what?"

She flinched and put a glare on his attorney, who briefly whispered something in Perry's ear. Perry grumbled, accepted the document from the bailiff and furiously scribbled his name.

The bailiff walked it over to Tiffany. She signed it as well, then breathed a sigh of relief as she looked over at Dwayne, who smiled.

"So, we're all done here?" Tiffany asked, getting to her feet and extending her hand to Dwayne, who captured it.

"Yes, you are," replied the judge.

Everyone gathered their things and made their way toward the door.

"Mr. Richards," the judge said, causing everyone to put their focus on her. "I meant Ms. Richards is all done here. You, are not." She gestured to the bailiff. "Take him into custody."

"Wait! What?!" Perry shook his head as the bailiff took out a pair of handcuffs.

"Falsifying records and submitting them to the Court is a crime. You're going to spend a little time as a guest of the Cook County Jail."

"You can't do that," he screeched, backing towards the door.

"I can. And I will. That's only fair, right?"

Perry did a two-step and broke out in a sprint. Dwayne slid in, blocking his path. Perry pushed forward, but was unable to move Dwayne out of the way. "Isn't evading arrest another charge, Your Honor?" Dwayne asked.

Perry froze at those words. He glanced over his shoulder at the judge, whose red lips lifted in a smile. "It most certainly is."

"And um ... that could keep him there long enough for Ms. Richards to sell the property and bring the court the documentation and proceeds for the split." Dwayne wiggled his eyebrows. "That's only fair, right?"

"You know, young man," she said, waving the gavel. "I love the way you think."

She banged the gavel and said. "Take him away."

CHAPTER 24

"Brothers, I need your help. We need your help." Dwayne inhaled and released it slowly as he walked into the Castle's boardroom. "These young men, my scholars, took on a monumental task alone. They did well for what they could accomplish on their own. But now, we need to step in and finish things up so they can focus on being scholars once again."

Miguel, Dylan, and the rest of their crew stood not too far from the entrance. Dwayne beckoned them to come closer. They complied and fanned out to the empty spaces around the boardroom table.

"What do you need?" Jai asked, his shock of silver hair shining under the glow of the lights.

Dwayne filled the Kings in on what Miguel had told them about Eduardo, Caesar, New Calvary, and the pastor. He also explained the condition of the building they had been evicted from. As well as what the scholars had been able to pull together temporary housing for the senior citizens.

"Well, how many seniors are we talking?" Reno asked, leaning back in his chair.

Dwayne shifted his gaze to Miguel, who said, "About seventy-five.

They're not sickly or anything like that. They just don't have the money to live somewhere else. The building receives government funds for each one of them."

"And that means it'll take time for the funds to redirect to a new place," Jai said as Reno nodded. They both ran centers which also had to maneuver around government red tape.

"Well, that's too many to put up in one of my shelters," Reno offered with a weary sigh.

"What about your father's estate?" Grant asked him over the rim of his wineglass.

Reno ran a hand through his dark hair and thought about that for a moment. "After what happened with him not keeping my confidence regarding my clients last time, I don't use his property for anything."

"What about the Castle," Shaz suggested. "That has plenty of room."

"Why didn't I think of that?" Vikkas asked

"Because it's too close to home," Daron said, grimacing. "Having all those little old people rolling around, playing cards—"

"Sneaking into each other's rooms," Jai chimed in, grinning.

"Hey," Dwayne warned, holding up a hand. "I don't need a mental picture. Seniors aren't into all that."

"Says you," Grant taunted as the rest of them laughed. "Remember Jai's mother and father are—"

"Hey-hey-hey," Vikkas said, holding his hand up to halt whatever else was coming down the line.

"I definitely don't need a mental picture of that," Jai said. "But I'm telling you, do not rule out the geriatric club."

"So, that's the plan?" Dwayne asked. "There are nine wings in the residential part of the Castle, but there are the guest suites in the part of the building near the bridge."

"But then we're going to have a bigger problem," Daron said.

Dwayne scratched his head. "What?"

"They move in," Vikkas mentioned. "They're not going to want to move back into their old apartments."

"That's a great point," Grant said. "We have to do something about that building they lived in."

"Truthfully, we need to put a torch to it," Miguel grumbled.

"That bad, eh?" Daron said, fingering the brim of his fedora.

Miguel stepped forward. "They haven't done anything to that place since before my abuelita came. The church brought Mr. Wilson in to make things better. All he did was take the money. Then he put them out when I had Mr. Sanchez came into the mix. I made a mistake there. I should have come to Mr. Harper, but I …" His gaze lowered to the carpet.

"It's all right," Dwayne said, placing an arm about Miguel's shoulders. The other scholars came forward as a show of solidarity. "I'm here now," Dwayne said. "*We're* here now and *we* will figure this all out." He looked to his fellow Kings who all nodded or gave some sign of agreement. "That's all that matters."

CHAPTER 25

A chair crashed through the front window of Miguel's house and landed on the porch just as Dwayne raised his foot to step on the bottom stair.

His shoes crunched shards of glass when he dashed toward the petrified teen standing behind an on old futon on the far side of the porch.

"Get down, Miguel!" Dwayne caught hold of the teen's sleeve and pulled him to the ground. A bullet flew past sixteen-year-old Miguel's shoulder and penetrated a worn wooden column of the porch.

"Miguel, run. Now!"

Dwayne hit the remote start button as they raced to the car and scrambled inside. He threw his Audi into gear. The smell of burning rubber filled the air when he peeled off down the street.

Miguel struggled to pull the seat belt across his chest, then blew out a loud breath when it clicked shut.

"Why didn't you warn me that he had a gun?" Dwayne asked, making a right at Roosevelt and Pulaski. When he received an urgent text from Miguel asking for help, nothing in him was prepared to come upon a scene that required him to duck and dodge gunfire. "Were you just going to let me walk in there and get shot?"

Miguel shook his head so hard Dwayne thought it would fall off. "No, sir, Mr. Harper," he said, glancing out of the rearview mirror. "I swear I didn't know he was going to do this. He's been ticked off ever since he found out about Eduardo Sanchez. And today, he just flipped out about the whole thing. Are you going to call the police?"

"I'm going to call someone even better," Dwayne answered.

He hit the button on his steering wheel and said, "Dial Daron."

A cheerful voice answered. "Harp, what's happening, man? Don't hear from you all month, now it's twice in one week."

"I have an emergency and I need your help." He sped up to keep from getting stopped at a light that was changing from yellow to red.

His brother's voice turned solemn. "What's going on?"

"I tried to help a scholar out and almost took a bullet."

"Where are you?" Daron's voice mirrored the urgency in Dwayne's.

"Just turned off Pulaski onto Cermak. Lou Malnati's is about four blocks away on Ogden. I'll pull over in the parking lot."

"Reno's a lot closer to you than I am right now."

"Doesn't matter. I might need more than one of you. That fool was so trigger happy he almost took out his own son."

"I'll be there in twenty," Daron said, fingers tap dancing on the keyboard.

CHAPTER 26

"Your son could've been killed," Dwayne roared as Reno, Daron, and Dro closed ranks around him at Miguel's house. "And it would have all been your fault."

"Dwayne, let's keep this civil," Daron warned.

Miguel's stepfather Antonio Maldonado moved in, trying to intimidate Dwayne. "You don't come here tellin' me nothin' about that boy. You ride around in your fancy car and expensive suits, thinkin' you better than me."

Those words, first spoken by Perry weeks ago, and now this coward, seemed to be the insecure man's mantra.

Antonio pointed at Dwayne's chest. Reno stepped forward, slid between them and pressed into the man's pudgy finger, moving him backward.

Dwayne nodded at Reno. "Stand down, bro. I've got this."

Reno didn't move. Instead, Antonio cursed under his breath and opened the can of beer in his hand.

"You won't put any effort into making sure your son doesn't fail," Dwayne said. "But you want to fight the man who tries to look out for the son you didn't even acknowledge until he started to make something of himself?"

"He's my stepson," the man growled, moving to the couch, taking a seat, and tossing back a gulp of beer. "And I'll raise him the way I see fit." He nodded as though agreeing with his own logic because no one else would. "I'll raise him."

Dro tilted his head and narrowed his gaze at Antonio. "But what does that have to do with you trying to put a bullet in my brother?"

"Just tryin' to scare him off, that's all," Antonio replied, eyes darting from one man to the other. "Here lately, all I hear from that boy is 'Mr. Harper says this. Mr. Harper says that.' I'm the one puttin' food in his belly and a roof over his head. The way he runs around here praisin' you is disrespectful to me."

"I'm not trying to disrespect you," Dwayne said. "But your son was this close"—he moved his index finger toward his thumb—"to being shot today. By his own stepfather. And he was just as close to shooting a man a couple months ago. He could've gone to jail."

"You shoulda let him. I don't care what happens to him anymore. First, he had you on a pedestal. Then he let that politician man brainwash him into thinking he was his real father. So, I guess in his eyes, I'm not doing anything for him." He sneered at Miguel. "Ungrateful son of—"

Daron shifted to move in, but Dwayne held up a hand to stall him for a moment.

"Jail woulda made the boy man up," Antonio said. "Instead, he walkin' around dreamin' about goin' to law school. I ain't had no fancy schoolin', and I made it in the world." He gave his stepson a disdainful onceover. "He's so dumb, he'll be lucky if he makes it through high school."

Antonio scowled at the silent foursome whose glares were almost tangible. "You book-smart people ain't got no street smarts. And that boy is so ignorant that he ain't got book or street smarts."

Dwayne looked at Miguel, who had tears in his eyes.

Antonio continued his tirade. "The streets will chew him up and spit him out if he keeps listenin' to a soft-handed pup like you."

"And I'm here to tell you that street smarts can only get you so far," Dwayne shot back. He flickered a gaze to Miguel. "Your son has a better start in life than you or I did because I'm making sure he lives out his potential and not your pain."

Reno, Daron, and Dro shared a glance and a slight nod.

Miguel wiped away a tear and tried to smile.

"Miguel has made straight A's ever since I started mentoring and tutoring him a year ago," Dwayne admitted, placing an arm around Miguel's shoulder, a move that seemed to anger Antonio even more. He twisted his lips and gave a phony round of applause. "Guess that's why him and my old lady act like they ain't got no need for me. They got you."

"Is that why she looks weary and is always walking on eggshells?" Daron asked, drawing on information that Miguel had told them when they all met up at the pizza place.

"It's nothing like that," Antonio growled.

"Yeah, it was exactly like that," Miguel confessed, finding his voice and the courage to stop living by the "what happens in this house stays in this house" code. "You control everyone in this house. You tell her when to breathe, when to blink, and she does it because she's scared."

Antonio glowered angrily at them. "Ain't none of this your business. I'm the husband. I'm the father. You stay out of that boy's life." He waggled a finger at Dwayne. "He ain't got no need for that fancy Excel place no more. I'll teach him whatever he needs to know in life."

Dwayne parted his lips to speak, but Reno stepped in front of him. "Look at you," he said to Antonio. "So bitter you can't even man up and give your son and wife the security they deserve. Your son needs someone like my brother because you have no clue how smart Miguel truly is." Dwayne shook his head. "I see your type all the time. Normally the women they're supposed to love end up in domestic violence shelters because that love can land them in an early grave."

"I wouldn't kill my wife," Antonio protested.

"But you're killing your son," Daron protested. "And we are not going to stand by and watch it happen."

Reno faced Miguel. "Go get your mother and sister. Have her gather up whatever she can't do without. You too."

"What for?" Antonio asked, eyes wide with alarm as he scrambled to his feet.

"They are coming with us," Daron said. "Since you don't know how to treat them, we're going to take them to a safe place.

"You can't just come in here and take my wife, my daughter and that boy," he whined.

"Why not?" Dwayne shot back. "You don't take care of her or the kids. We will."

Antonio moved to put hands on Daron, then shifted to pull out a gun. All four of the men had their weapons out in the time it took to blink.

Dwayne walked over, pushed the man further into the sofa, and leaned over in Antonio's face. "Now we can do this the hard way, or ..."

CHAPTER 27

All eyes were on Chanel Bordeaux the moment she stepped into the Gala.

In keeping with the "You Are Royalty" theme of the event, the Excel Charter School Ensemble played a few bars of a smooth jazz piece they'd composed, then the trumpets heralded her arrival as the words "Please welcome Miss Chanel Bordeaux" floated through the speakers.

She gave a "Miss America wave". Her black velvet mermaid gown elegantly skimmed over a body that could grace a Victoria's Secret catalogue. The tiny rhinestones in her strapless dress sparkled like stars in a midnight sky. From her diamond tiara to her long black satin gloves, the woman personified the "You Are Royalty" theme of the event. A metallic balloon arrangement spelled out 'Excel'. Floating candles on the tables added a touch of elegance.

The eight women, who were the mates of Dwayne's King brothers, were situated around the room, helping in various aspects of the Gala, under the direction of the scholars. These women, who were amazing in their own right, were fast becoming Tiffany's friends. Over the past few weeks, they'd met for lunch and vibed about what the Kings were doing and how they should follow suit with endeavors that complemented the

Castle's purpose. Tiffany was all for it, and had also been asked for input when it came to Jai's rehabilitation center and other health centers he planned to open under the Knights' direction.

Instead of heading straight to Dwayne's side, Tiffany remained near the back entrance off the parking lot and watched Chanel from across the room. Tiffany's off-the shoulder black tulle gown was embellished with pearls and had been specifically picked out by Dwayne because she couldn't decide on what to wear for such a grand occasion. A tux was standard equipment for men, but women had an array of never-ending choices.

Khalil whispered something to Dwayne which made him frown before signaling for someone to bring over a wireless microphone. He passed it to Khalil, who said, "A peaceful evening to all."

The voices tricked to a halt and then replies of good evening echoed throughout the room.

"My apologies for having to leave so soon when my son and his scholars have put this magnificent affair together," Khalil said, scanning the expectant faces of the supporters. "A family emergency has arisen, but I wanted to be sure to give my blessing to Dwayne Harper, who is a man who shares a passion for learning"—his gaze swept to Tiffany, who inched back toward the door—"and loving. And it's reflected in this very room. All of you are here for one cause; to further the education plans of the scholars—prince and princesses of the Castle. That is admirable, and while I won't be here to see the final tally, I am certain more dollars will walk out of your purses and pockets and end up right at that table over … there."

He gestured to the spot where Camilla, Lola, Temple, and Autumn were accepting cash, checks, or charge from donors. Cameron, Skyler, Zuri, and Milan were handling the silent auction. "So, please, know that I'm not saying give until hurts, but I would like for you to at least say 'ouch'."

Dwayne roared with laughter, which was mirrored by his brothers and the rest of the audience. He accepted an embrace and the mic from Khalil, who placed his arm about his wife's waist and guided her from the room.

"That's my mentor, everyone," Dwayne said, beaming as he nodded in Khalil's direction. Pointing the microphone toward the jazz ensemble, he said, "Maestro, take it away."

The music came back on at the same moment that conversations and laughter resumed.

Looking like a queen surveying her kingdom, Chanel's eyes roamed the space. Only when the trumpets sounded again, and the announcer welcomed the couple behind her did Chanel descend the entryway stairs.

The Ensemble finished their song and a tuxedo-clad scholar stepped to the podium. "Mr. Harper, would you come onstage for a moment please?" he asked, imitating an Idris Elba British accent.

Chanel seemed to have found her target when Dwayne came from behind the curtains. She glided to the stairs beside the stage and stood at the bottom step. As the crowd of standing people applauded Dwayne, Chanel looked at him with adoration. Several people moved toward him when he turned towards the stairs. Chanel had already positioned herself so that she would be the first person he encountered when he came down.

He paused, searching the room for something, and then grimacing.

Tiffany remained in her obscure spot.

Chanel stepped up and gave Dwayne a hug that lasted just a little too long for Tiffany's liking. Dwayne gently moved her away from him, but the woman attached herself to him again, this time whispering something in his ear.

The peck on the cheek that followed was all Tiffany needed to see to confirm her suspicions that Chanel was still on the hunt. "Lord Jesus, give me strength," she prayed in a soft voice. "But not too much, or else I might break that woman's neck."

Jai, Vikkas, and Kaleb, three of Dwayne's brother Kings, came forward and slowly inched themselves between Chanel and Dwayne. Two others—Grant and Shaz—flanked him.

Tiffany kept her eyes on her prey as she left her spot to make it to the other side of the room. She was stopped along the way.

"Miss Tiffany, did you see the trophy we got Mr. Harper?" Miguel looked like a total grown-up in his black tuxedo, even though his eyes carried the excitement of a child at Christmas.

"I sure did. He was really surprised, wasn't he?" She patted his shoulder. "He's so proud of you guys, and so am I." Glancing in Dwayne's direction, she added, "Excuse me please, Miguel. I need to speak with Mr. Harper."

"Okay, Miss Tiffany." He waved to a couple of his classmates and motioned for them to meet him at the buffet, a spread fit for kings, queens, princes, and princesses. Oh, and a court jester, if she could give Chanel a title.

Tiffany continued toward Dwayne. He noticed her when she was a few yards away. His smile warmed her heart—and obviously cooled Chanel's heels. The woman grimaced at Tiffany then instantly replaced her smirk with a pasted-on smile when Dwayne looked her way.

The Kings greeted Tiffany warmly, embracing her before dispersing among the attendees, aiming to make it toward the tables where their women were situated. Dro and Daron gave Dwayne a look over their shoulders that Tiffany couldn't decipher. One of them gestured toward a distinguished gentlemen in the center of the ballroom who was surrounded by several politicians who had sought out an invitation at the last minute. Dwayne nodded, then put his gaze on Chanel and asked, "You remember Tiffany, don't you?"

"I do," she replied, adjusting her chiffon wrap.

Dwayne placed a kiss on her lips. "I didn't expect to see you here."

"Oh well, you know us women are full of surprises." She winked at Chanel, whose sour expression said she hadn't expected to see Tiffany either.

Chanel placed a hand on Dwayne's broad chest. "I wanted to tell you how impressed I am with the work you've done with these boys. Watching the impact you've had on their lives has made me want to do more to help young people." She moved a little closer, trying to inch Tiffany out of the way. "I had a dream the other night, and I think God was telling me to open up a youth center or something. Do you think you could assist me?" She flirted with her eyes, totally ignoring Tiffany's presence.

"Give me a minute to run over here and get us something to drink," he said, plucking her hands from his chest and pressing a kiss to Tiffany's cheek.

"I'd like an orgasm please." Chanel said, looking at him and raising an eyebrow. She covered her mouth in mock modesty. "It's a drink made with amaretto, Kahlúa, and Baileys Irish Cream."

"Then I'll take 'Death in the afternoon,'" Tiffany replied. "Some of us need it more than others."

Dwayne laughed. "You sound like you want to kill someone."

"No one in particular," she said, eyeing Chanel. "Death in the afternoon is a drink made from a shot of absinthe and champagne."

"Well, I hate to disappoint you ladies, but there's no alcohol at this event." He pinned a gaze on Tiffany. "And what do you know about a Death in the Afternoon? You don't even drink." He chuckled. "I'll be back with some soft drinks. Emphasis on the word soft."

"Good. Us girls will chat until you get back," Tiffany said as he maneuvered between couples on the dance floor swaying to the Ensemble's music and his brother followed suit.

Chanel growled. "You're not even supposed to be here." Her tone was like fire but her expression was pure ice. "Don't you get it? He's done with you."

"Says who?"

"Dwayne. You couldn't tell that he didn't expect to see you here?"

Tiffany reached out and gently pushed aside a lock of hair that had come loose from Chanel's elegant updo. She then leaned in and whispered, "Since you seem to be interviewing for the position of the future Mrs. Dwayne Harper, I just thought I'd fix your hair so you can look your best when he tells you the position is already taken."

Tiffany stepped back, and Dwayne moved in. He handed her a glass of sparkling grape juice and said, "No fair. I want you to whisper in my ear too." He nibbled her ear and planted a kiss on her cheek.

She relished the red color creeping up Chanel's face.

"I don't understand," the woman protested. "First you were surprised to see her, now you can't keep your hands off her. She's your ex for crying out loud."

Dwayne's head snapped to Tiffany with confusion etched on his face. He handed Chanel a drink, then hooked his free arm around Tiffany's waist. "I don't know where you're getting your misinformation. She's not my ex. She's my future wife. In fact, she graciously agreed to move the wedding up by three months."

He gazed at Tiffany before finishing his response. "And the reason I was surprised to see her was because Tiffany volunteered to pick up a scholar's parent from work, take her home to change clothes, and then bring her here. I didn't think she'd make it back in time."

Dwayne waggled a finger at Tiffany when he said, "You don't have any speeding tickets I need to know about, do you, young lady?"

She smiled up at him. "Given the distance I had to drive, I thought the Gala would be over by now."

Chanel opened her small purse and poured a clear liquid from a silver flask into her glass before downing it in one swallow.

"Then I guess she didn't tell you, huh?"

"Tell me what?" Dwayne asked, frowning.

"Now I know she didn't tell you, because if she had, you would have dropped her like a hot potato," she said between her teeth. "I told you he's too good a man to be with someone like you who keeps secrets the way you do. And I warned you that if you didn't tell him the truth, I would."

Dwayne flickered a gaze between the two. "What is she talking about, Tiffany?"

"You didn't know that she has a child, did you?" Chanel asked. "And worse than that, she disowned that child from the day it was born. A man who loves children the way you do deserves a woman like me who can help him in his professional endeavors." She looked Tiffany up and down. "You can't do that." Chanel let out a deep breath, satisfied that she had landed a blow.

"Chanel, you're an enterprising woman," Dwayne began in a patient tone he normally reserved for misbehaving scholars.

She drew close to his side. He moved away and pulled Tiffany in front of him, wrapping his arms around her waist and bringing her close. "But Tiffany has already told me everything." He kissed her hair. "And the day she was brave enough to trust me with that knowledge is the day I fell more in love with her than I ever thought I could."

"So, like I said," Tiffany began. "You can quit interviewing for the position of future Mrs. Dwayne Harper. It's. Been. Filled."

"And this beautiful woman will never retire, quit, or get fired. So, your services aren't needed in my life, Chanel. I never took you up on anything you offered. So why would you think my love life would be any different?" He gestured toward the exit. "You might want to make use of that door right there."

CHAPTER 28

"We have a problem," Dro whispered to Dwayne.

Dwayne's head swiveled toward Dro, whose gaze was focused across the room at a tall, distinguished man wearing a designer tuxedo and a plastered-on smile.

Both men displayed poker faces. It wouldn't be good to let the people around them know of the danger in their midst. Dwayne and his King brothers had been working nonstop behind the scenes to identify the man behind the failed attempt on Khalil's life. Avenging their mentor and sending a message to anyone else wanting to get him out of the picture was a top priority.

"Our takedown of the mastermind has been moved up," Dro added, glancing at his cell. "Daron received some intel that the guy's trying to catch a plane out tonight."

Dwayne leaned toward Tiffany. "Something has come up that we need to take care of, love. We'll meet you and the other ladies in the parlor at the Castle when we return." He planted a kiss on her lips.

"Is there something I can do to help?"

"Are you packing?"

"I left it at home," she said before he turned to follow Dro into the crowd.

He whipped back around. "Wait a minute. I was joking. You carry a weapon?"

"You don't?" she shot back.

Dro guided him forward into the crowd. Dwayne looked back at Tiffany, whose expression showed she was ready to smile.

"Mr. Harper," said a petite woman who touched Dwayne's arm, causing him and Dro to stall for a moment. The silver braid knotted atop her head gave her an additional three inches in height. "This was a wonderful evening. I hope we can speak more about your future plans."

"I would love that," he replied, spotting Dr. Fowler, who also had been stopped on the way out the door by one of the men who had crowded around him earlier. "But right now, I need to speak with someone before he leaves." Dwayne angled so he could make a dash for it if it came to that. "Please contact me at Excel and we'll set something up."

Dwayne excused himself before she could detain him any longer. He weaved through the throng of bodies until he reached his target. "Dr. Fowler, how did you enjoy the Gala?"

"A perfect night." The man's smile widened as if he had been awarded a million-dollar prize, and maybe as far as he knew, he had. Inroads had been made to infiltrate the Castle's medical facility in order to retrieve some of the work, treatments, and serums he had left behind.

Jai and the Knights had finally finished the inventory on the place and everything became clear. While everyone had their eyes on all the other crimes tied to the Castle, ranging from sex trafficking, to drugs, illegal adoption, and unwilling organ donors, they hadn't given a thought to the fact that the medical facility's vaults housed things so valuable that they couldn't have a price put on them. Well, the good doctor had found a way to put a price on them and he had every intention of cashing in.

Dr. Fowler was very much aware that the place was a virtual intellectual property gold mine. He had hired men to take out Khalil before the meeting with eight of his former mentees, and the subsequent transfer of Castle ownership, could take place. He had failed, and the Kings had come in, cleaned house and put any remaining enemies on notice—the Kings would do everything in their power to protect Khalil, the Castle, and the women they loved. Somehow, Dwayne had been able to comb through all of the data that his brothers had analyzed. Dr. Fowler might have been the person who hired the muscle and trigger, but the inside track on how Dr. Fowler had managed to get so close to Khalil in the first place, that was someone else's doing. But who?

"I wanted to talk to you more about the advancements of the Castle's medical facility. Jai was telling me how cutting edge they were." Dwayne watched Dro in the foyer discreetly take out one of Fowler's security guards, stuffing him in a nearby closet. "Several of my students could benefit from a talk on some of the medical discoveries you've made."

"Unfortunately, while I'd love to help the little charter school you're so invested in," Fowler said, retrieving a cell from his suit jacket pocket then glancing at the screen. "I have a higher calling that requires me to be overseas for the next few years."

"Well, I'd love to schedule something before you leave." Dwayne saw Daron's motion for him to keep Dr. Fowler talking.

"Speaking of leaving. Mr. Harper, have a wonderful rest of the evening. I know I will," Dr. Fowler chuckled. He patted Dwyane on the back.

Dwayne didn't like the tone of that comment and he trailed the doctor out, joining his brothers in the foyer.

"The Knights will handle the Gala's wrap up," Jai announced as they left the building.

"What did he say that has you frowning like that?" Vikkas asked, keeping in step with Dwayne.

"It's not what he said. It's the way he said it that disturbed me."

Dwayne scanned the area, noticing that Shaz, Dro, and Grant weren't among the Kings present at the Gala. "Where did Dro and the others go?"

"They're getting into position. We have to reach Dr. Fowler's convoy to slow it down and make sure our guys have enough time to get to the hangar," Daron replied as they neared the car. "Your conversation bought us some time. We just need a little more." He slid into the passenger side.

Dwayne started the vehicle as Jai, Vikkas, Reno, and Kaleb pulled off in separate rides.

"What slip up let you know who it was and when they planned their next step?" Dwayne asked as he trailed Kaleb's SUV. Something major had to have happened for them to be activating everything tonight instead of the following evening as originally planned.

"Earlier this evening, Dr. Fowler handed Najan some paperwork," Daron answered.

Najan Maharaj was Khalil's brother. He had squandered his portion of the family fortune, and now wanted to take control of the wealth of the Castle. In his eyes, the Castle had been started with Maharaj monies and those funds should be returned to the family coffers—in his pocket to be exact.

Daron retrieved a tablet from his inner pocket. "When I heard Dr. Fowler tell Najan he'd be out of the country with an airtight alibi and ready to push the button on turning billions into trillions, I knew what was happening. They were getting ready to force Khalil into signing over the rights to the pharmaceutical products at the Castle."

"Do they really think we'd let him get away with it?" Dwayne asked maneuvering behind a grey Tesla sandwiched between two black Suburbans.

"Khalil was suddenly called away for a family issue," Dro said over the coms. "That isn't a coincidence."

Dwayne had always said Khalil's family was behind a great deal of the Castle's troubles.

"Remember, once they grid them in, make sure they can't get around," Daron said into the communication device linked to the other Kings' vehicles.

Jai pulled in front of the lead SUV as Vikkas and Reno drove alongside the grey Tesla. Dwayne and Kaleb pulled along either side of the last SUV. Jai's speed dropped to the actual limit. The Black SUV tried to push Jai's vehicle off the road.

Dwayne swerved on to the shoulder as the Suburban next to him continued to merge into his other lane. The idea wasn't to get into an accident. Just force them to slow down, especially since the traffic was light at this time.

"Switch positions," Daron called out.

Reno picked up speed, heading in front of Jai and effectively giving Dwayne his spot. The Suburban was forced into a position behind Dwayne.

"How long do we need to delay him?" Dwayne watched as Jai dropped back, riding next to Dr. Fowler's Tesla.

"Another quarter of a mile and the team should have enough of a head start to get in position."

The Kings shifted places again. Dwayne glanced at the clock on the dashboard, realizing his next move was now. "I'm peeling off."

CHAPTER 29

Dwayne pulled ahead, made his move around Reno as Kaleb took his spot alongside the Tesla. He and Daron needed to arrive a few minutes ahead of Dr. Fowler to put the cameras in place. He tucked the vehicle between the hangar's side entrance and a service truck, and took out a device called the Emperor's Suit that Daron handed him on their way to their vehicles. Dwayne put it on and turned it on before leaving the car.

The device had been a top-secret invention that several governments had tried to kill the inventor to obtain. It rendered the wearer the ability to be "invisible" to the naked eye, something Dwayne and Daron needed at the moment to make it onto that private plane without alerting the guards.

They sprinted down the tarmac, knowing the director was only minutes behind them.

"Do you think we'll be ready?" Dwayne didn't like that law enforcement wasn't already situated around the area like they originally intended. Almost every plan the Kings had executed before now meant they called in the most trustworthy of the appropriate authorities to ensure that those who had come against the Castle would be brought to justice. Well, that is, after the Kings had administered their own brand of justice as a going-away present.

"Dro made sure the plane is grounded," Daron answered. "We just have to keep him here and running his mouth until Jason Stone and his agents arrives."

"Cameron's brother has probably seen enough of us and the Castle to last him a lifetime," Dwayne replied referring to the FBI agent and brother to Daron's queen, who they called whenever they took on the corrupt elements that had infiltrated the Castle.

"He's been catching flack for being on some of these cases that aren't in his jurisdiction," Daron said. "But as long as he shows up, we know things won't get mired in government red tape and the bad boys can't buy their way out of prison."

Dwayne trotted behind Daron toward the private plane. "We definitely can't allow these men back on the street."

They quieted while walking past the two security guards standing at the base of the plane's stairs.

Dwayne remained out of the view of the door and the camera that Daron secured in brackets above the entrance. He pulled out and placed a clip onto his tie which would also videotape what occurred, then replaced his cuff links with a pair that had recording capabilities. These were also inventions of his tech guru brother. The remaining Kings would be watching from nearby in case they needed to assist.

This wasn't the only time Dwayne was grateful that Khalil had insisted that every scholar at Macro learn basic weaponry and self-defense. Every single one. Despite the seriousness of the moment, he chuckled, wondering if Milan, Vikkas' queen, had missed a few sessions. They still had occasion to question her aim the day she had to shoot her brother for holding her hostage. Khalil had always said he was of two philosophies. Peace when feasible. Kick ass and take names when necessary. A perfect blend of Martin Luther King and the early teachings of Malcolm X.

Grant's voice came over the coms. "Dr. Fowler should be your way in five."

As predicted, Dr. Fowler entered the luxurious cabin, holding only a black briefcase with two of his security guards trailing him. He looked at Grayson Daniels, a plant from Dro, who came from the rear of the plane carrying a tray with a glass of scotch on it. "You're new."

"I'm the emergency replacement for Carl. Sahara is in the back setting up your room sir," Grayson responded as Dr. Fowler accepted the drink and seemed to relax a the mention of his normal attendant's name. "Do you need anything else?"

"Tell the pilot to get this bird in the air." Dr. Fowler loosened his tie, placing the briefcase next to his chair. "I'm not coming back until the paperwork is in order."

"Will do." Grayson walked to the cockpit, knocking before entering.

Dwyane turned off The Emperor's device and came into view. "I don't think we finished our conversation," he said to Dr. Fowler.

Dr. Fowler startled and the glass slipped from his hand. His head whipped around, trying to place what had transpired as the fiery liquid spread onto his slacks and dripped to the carpet. He shifted his attention in Dwayne's direction as the guards shared a quick glance before they left their seats and whipped out their guns.

"I wouldn't do that if I was you," Dro said, smiling as he emerged from the back with Grant, weapons drawn.

Daron, still under the Emperor's Suit cloaking, removed the Glocks from the guards' hands. They staggered backward, eyes bucked wide as they looked at their guns seemingly hanging in thin air.

"It doesn't matter if I fly out now or tomorrow." Dr. Fowler leaned back in the chair, displaying a cocky smile. "Things are already in place. I will still get what I want and there's nothing you can do to stop it. You can't take away what I know, gentlemen. And you can't protect everyone at once."

"But we can put you away for a long time," Dro fired back, sharing a glance with Dwayne. Probably at how calm the man was with this much opposition surrounding him.

"You have no proof I did anything not tied to my job before parting ways with the Castle," Dr. Fowler said, glaring at Dro, who was pouring another glass of scotch and taking a sip. "Wasn't it your security team that dragged me out. So, what is this really about?"

"Brother, do you want to show him what we have?" Dwayne looked at Daron.

An image projected in front of Dr. Fowler caused that cocky smile to disappear. The day he set up the assassination with Gino Greer, the man he had hired to take Khalil's life, played in full damning display.

"What was that about proof?" Dro roared with satisfaction in his tone. "Evidently, the shooters wanted you to ensure you upheld your end of the deal."

Shaz sauntered out of the cockpit, which signaled Jason Stone and his agents had arrived.

Dr. Fowler's normal cocky grin didn't return. Instead, it had been slowly replaced with an evil snarl. "Well, you have one part of the equation correct. I commend you." He checked his watch before obeying Agent Stone's command to stand. "You left the Original King of the Castle unprotected." His smile widened. "My condolences."

CHAPTER 30

"Khalil's in trouble."

The words caught Tiffany's attention, causing her to move closer to the open door where Cameron Stone stood talking to a handsome tall blond man with blue eyes. Nicco Wolfe was a member of Khalil's personal security team.

"Khalil's in a meeting with Najan and both the Maharaj and Bhandari families," Nicco replied as he peered down the hall. "I don't understand why Khalil's family would converge on the Castle all at once."

"Why is it only you left here to secure everything?" Cameron asked, staring in the same direction as Nicco. "The Maharaj and Bhandari families brought several armed men with them. There has to be a reason for that. They're expecting to intimidate him or something. This is not acceptable."

Tiffany peeked out but couldn't see what held their attention, so she stepped out of sight as they turned back.

"There was a disturbance on the grounds," Nicco explained, glancing at the tablet in his hand. "I had to send out a team to secure everything."

"With Daron and the Kings out, you're short-staffed." Cameron placed her hands into the waistband of the peach ball gown that graced her womanly curves in such a way that Daron had insisted on a little … *pickle tickle* before they made it to the Gala.

"We have a team on its way," Nicco assured.

"They'll be too late. The Kings are handling something that came up concerning the former medical director of this place. The Knights are making sure the scholars from the Gala make it home safely." Cameron leaned in saying something in a low whisper that Tiffany couldn't make out.

Nicco handed her the tablet. "I take it you're running point?"

"I am. I'm not getting a good feeling about this. Based on what I overheard, they're trying to force Khalil to sign something over to them. And it's related to Dr. Fowler somehow." Cameron and Nicco spoke in hushed tones before Cameron said, "Let's get moving. I don't know how much more talking will be done before things turn ugly." She nodded for Nicco to follow her toward the parlor.

Tiffany scurried away from the door and into the safety of the parlor. Her heart pounded in her chest. Soon Cameron called out to her. She had also collected Milan, Zuri, Temple, Skyler, Autumn, Camilla, and Lola along the way.

"Ladies, Khalil is in a dangerous position," Cameron said, pacing until she stood in the center of the women who were grouped in the middle of the room. "We all know the men in our lives will be crushed to pieces if they return and something has happened to him."

What did Cameron expect them to do? Tiffany searched the other women's faces in the room who were all still in their elegant evening gowns, and their faces all mirrored what she felt.

"How can we help?" Zuri asked, twirling the gold bracelet on her arm.

"I'm going to need you, Autumn, and Lola to go to the security room to watch the monitors and report any suspicious activity to me. It'll free up more men to protect the grounds." Cameron handed her watch to Autumn. "If anyone gets close, slam down on the face of the watch. It'll tase them."

"Aren't we just watching monitors?" Autumn frowned attaching the watch to her wrist.

"Yes, but I don't want to leave you unprotected, either." Cameron shifted her crossbody to the front of her.

"What about me?" Zuri asked, her dark skin glowing under the dim lighting. "Should I get something as well?"

Tiffany watched as Nicco stepped back toward the entrance. The other ladies gathered near Cameron as she pulled out a fat pen from her purse.

"You want me to write them off?" Zuri asked with her brow furrowed.

Cameron clicked the pen top and a knife dropped. "It's laced with a knock-out drug. Try not to cut yourself." She retracted the blade and handed the weapon to Zuri, then passed a black tube to Lola. She pressed the button and it extended to a full-length staff. Lola simply nodded her admiration.

"What about the rest of us?" Temple asked, scanning the faces of the women who hadn't been armed.

"Temple and Skyler will go with Nicco," Cameron answered. "He'll escort you to the armory for supplies before taking the others to the security room." They followed Nicco into the hallway.

Tiffany debated whether she should call Dwayne. Her thoughts were on all Khalil had done to help shape him into the man she loved. All of the Kings spoke on how grateful they were to him.

"What about me?" Tiffany asked as the two women trotted across the threshold.

Cameron's head whipped toward her. "Do you know how to handle a gun?"

"I'm from Texas," Tiffany shot back with a shrug.

Cameron simply stared at her and said, "And?"

"Of course I know how to shoot. And from what I hear, my aim is better than Milan's."

"I'm telling you," Milan said with a heavy sigh as she threw up her hands. "I missed on purpose."

"Camilla and Milan, I need you to run and grab some of the larger crossbody purses from your suites." Cameron stared at the screen of the tablet, then looked up at Tiffany as she slid out a gun tucked away in a hidden layer of her wide silk-covered waistband. "I need you to remain here for now."

"Doing nothing?" Tiffany questioned, incensed because she wanted to be useful.

"No." Cameron glanced at the door and across the hall. "Keeping an eye on the library for any additional activities. Use your cell to call me right away. Punch these digits in. But if it can't wait ... shoot first and ask questions, never."

Tiffany recalled seeing several men go into the library earlier. None of them had come out when Najan and the rest of the family arrived. When that happened, her first thought was, *What's the cause of this late-night visit from the family? Nothing good.*

Cameron handed Tiffany the tablet then lifted the peach material to retrieve a Ruger strapped to her inner thigh.

"How many of those darn things do you have?" Tiffany asked, shaking her head in disbelief.

"A woman can never have too much protection." She chuckled, then nodded to the hallway. "You can keep an eye on the rest of the corridor. If anyone other than Nicco or the ladies enter, get out of sight." She placed a hand over the gun in Tiffany's hand. "But use this if you have to."

"Okay," Tiffany said as she angled herself to have a better view of the library across the way.

Cameron slipped out into the hallway. On the tablet, Tiffany could see she was lingering outside the study just down the hallway that had an entrance which led into the library, then the parlor. Najan and two gentlemen had been escorted in by the Castle security team less than twenty minutes ago.

Tiffany kept her eye on the monitor, and flinched when the screen split into four different views of the Castle grounds. Cameron must have some way to control it remotely. Her mind shifted to thoughts of Khalil being murdered at the hands of his own family. Even worse, if Cameron also died in her attempt to save him.

CHAPTER 31

Tiffany said a silent prayer of protection to help calm her nerves.

Several minutes later, Cameron returned, followed by Skyler and Temple, who each carried a black duffel bag. "Tiffany, text Dwayne, tell him to call you whenever he can."

Contacting Dwayne had slipped her mind earlier. "Wouldn't it better if I called?" He'd want to know what was happening immediately.

"I want to give the Kings a heads up about what's going on here, but I don't want to distract them. They're knee deep in their own assignments right now. Dwayne will probably only contact you when it's safe." Cameron whipped her hair into a knot at the top of her head as Camilla and Milan reentered the parlor.

Tiffany's mind raced. Was Dwayne in danger too? She said another prayer for the Kings as she shot off the text and Cameron took a call.

"I just spoke with Daron," Cameron said. "Like I thought, they're too far away to get here in time. Here's the plan. We're going to interrupt the meeting." She nodded toward the Jamaican woman of the group. "Camilla, you'll be responsible for getting Aashna out as soon as an opportunity presents itself. Khalil will be less tethered if his wife is safe." She turned, focusing on Vikkas and Jai's women. "Milan and

Temple will secure the library." Then she finally put her gaze on the remaining two women. "Skyler, Tiffany, and I will focus on getting Khalil to safety."

"How are we going to help Khalil once we're inside?" Tiffany asked, moving until she stood next to Cameron. "There's a lot of people in there and only a few of us."

"By playing our part," Cameron answered, putting a short cylindrical device similar to the one she'd given Lola in a pocket in the shoulder of her dress.

"So, we will catch them off guard." Tiffany smiled.

"Exactly." Cameron laid out the rest of the plan as the women listened intently. "They'll assume by the way we're dressed that we're aren't armed and in no position to take them down." She took the crossbody purses and the weapons bag. "And that will be their mistake."

Cameron quickly explained how to use the gear she entrusted them with, then instructed on how to put them into the purses for easy retrieval. "Camilla and Skyler. Can you start with filling the empty glasses and place them on a tray?"

"Our way in," Skyler said, moving toward the bottles of red and white wine and others of sparkling grape juice that had been waiting to be cracked opened when the Kings made it back to the Castle.

"Celebrating a successful gala." Tiffany smiled at the brilliant simplicity of Cameron's plan. No overdone ruse planned by the queens of the Castle.

"Let me get Temple geared up, then Milan you're next," Cameron said. Walking over and clamping a device on the shoulder of Temple's dress, she pulled out two drones from the black bag. She did the same to Milan. "The drone will follow your movements and relay to Lola and those in the command center. One of them will let us know if you come across any problems."

Tiffany felt the energy in the room increase like a log ignited in a fireplace as Cameron passed out the weapons and communication devices. Tiffany listened carefully while Cameron went over the shield device instruction with her once again.

As much as she believed she could handle things, Tiffany realized she wasn't ready when she trailed Cameron across the hall to the library, and the woman entered the library firing several shots. Four men with assault rifles hit the floor with a solid thud.

Tiffany stifled a gasp. *Shoot first. Ask questions, never.*

"Were you going to let me get a shot in?" Tiffany asked Cameron who didn't bother to make eye contact as she replied, "Not if I can help it. I'm used to this. You're not."

Tiffany released a sigh of relief that Cameron didn't miss.

"Tiffany, know this. These men, they didn't come here to play. If it comes down to it, it'll be you or them. Shoot and we'll sort everything out later. Trust me on that." She spoke into the com and said. "Milan and Temple, the room is yours. Hold down the fort."

"We know what to do," they said in unison.

"Autumn, do you see them on the feed?" Cameron asked as the remaining women swept toward Khalil.

"Yes," the reply came in Tiffany's ear.

Camilla led the way with the tray of drinks. Tiffany kept touching the devices in her crossbody. "I can do this. I can do this." Her hands shook slightly as she ran her fingers over her hair.

"We got this," Cameron said, rubbing her shoulders.

Skyler knocked, then opened the door allowing Camilla to slip past her with the tray of drinks. "We thought we'd celebrate a night well done."

Najan quickly dropped his hand from in front of Khalil's face. "Now is not a good time," he growled. "We're discussing family business."

Khalil settled back in the chair, crossed one leg over the other as he peered closely at Cameron and smiled. Smooth. The man was unruffled.

"Khalil already said no to signing that ... that paperwork." Aashna sent a pointed glare Najan's way. "There's nothing else to say. And do not think we did not recognize that you have gone so far with your deception, that keep changing the variation of your name to avoid legal consequences. You are now Najan, when you have been Nayan all these years. And it keeps changing on the paperwork. What other reason is there for that?"

"Sounds like the discussion's over." Camilla glided past several chairs to where two men leaned on the mantel of the fireplace several feet away from Najan.

"Ladies, Khalil's ex-wife is heading your way," Zuri announced through the com.

"She looks ready to steam roll over someone," Lola added.

Tiffany heard her phone ringing in the purse and quickly silenced it.

Aashna smiled, cupping her hand around Khalil's face. "The Gala was beautiful tonight. The scholars—the princes as you called them—did such a wonderful job."

"Ladies," Najan said in a harsh tone, refusing the flute Camilla offered from the tray. "As I was saying, now is not the time!"

"No. Najan, I will not sign over the rights to the pharmaceutical products at the Castle." Khalil slid the paperwork back toward Najan. "Not under any circumstances. I realize that you and Dr. Fowler had some little plan all worked up. That is the reason I had asked Vikkas and the rest of my sons to come aboard. Those ... products housed in the medical facility cannot fall into the wrong hands." He gestured around them. "This place, the Castle, and everything it stands for, cannot fall into the wrong hands. Those nine men, and the men that they chose, and the teens, the scholars, the ... princes that they are mentoring—those are the right hands. People with the right heart, the right mind, the passion that will see things through."

Najan waved his fist in front of Khalil's face. "Do not make this more difficult than it has to be." The two men quickly flanked Najan's side.

"You're the one responsible for leaking Khalil's schedule that almost got him killed," Aashna accused Najan as she stood, gripping the arms of the chair for balance. "You evil man."

"It belonged under Maharaj control," Najan fired back as if that response cleared him of any wrongdoing. "Everything still has the Maharaj blood attached to it. He started this place with family money."

"I am not a Maharaj," Khalil argued. "They made sure of it when they stripped me of my name, my wife and one of my children. So, the Castle is not within the control of the Maharaj family. I made sure of that." Khalil's tone was calm and even as he rose from the plush chair, towering over Najan.

Najan whipped out a gun aiming at Aashna. "Sign the paperwork."

Tiffany's body went rigid. Things had escalated faster than she thought possible. Khalil's gaze flickered to Cameron, who tipped toward Camilla and whispered something in her ear before inching to the side until she was completely in front of Aashna. Skyler took the tray from Camilla, setting it on a small table nearby. Tiffany's heartrate went into overdrive as she reached a hand into the bag to grab the device so she would be ready. Three rapid knocks drew their attention.

"Yes," Khalil called out, his eyes never leaving Najan.

"Varsha Germaine here to see you," the male voice beyond the door announced.

"Send her in," Najan responded.

No one moved. Not a single soul. Khalil smiled and said, "It is fine. She can come."

Tiffany shifted nervously as the tension crackled in the room. Varsha stormed in, anger etched on her beautiful face. She had been Vikkas' mother for years. Until his wedding, when the duplicity behind the Maharaj family's actions came to light. Varsha had been the woman who had been foisted on Khalil as punishment for pursuing spiritual endeavors with his portion of the Maharaj fortune. Khalil had treated her with kindness and respect throughout the union, but love was something he only had for Aashna.

"I would not trust her either," Aashna warned, seconds before Camilla made eye contact with Khalil, who nodded as she maneuvered his beloved out the door to safety.

Skyler slowly inched toward the place where Tiffany stood.

"Did you really think I would let you have your happily ever after?" Varsha swept through the space as if she owned it. "You humiliated me. Stole everything from me. For these commoners. These half breeds and people who do not know what culture is."

"There are several men in the hidden passageway," Lola relayed through the coms with concern in her voice.

Tiffany pulled out the tablet. Cameron glanced at the screen from the drone to take in their position.

"And how are you going to stop me?" Khalil fired back as the two men with Najan moved forward to Khalil's side, trying to force him back into the seat. He remained in place, but his gaze went to Tiffany, who stiffened under his intense eyes. Cameron didn't make a move, so Tiffany remained in place.

"You did not think I would leave without making a ripple, did you?" She put a steely glare on Najan. "If I had known he was not up for the task of killing you, I would have handled it myself from the beginning. Looks like I still have to handle the business at hand," Varsha said as the hidden door behind the desk opened and eight men entered with weapons drawn.

One man bound Khalil's wrists as several other men moved in Najan's direction. The two men with Najan turned their weapons on Khalil.

"Do not let another person slip out of this room," Varsha said, her voice was laced with venom. "This ends tonight. You can keep your precious Castle. It's worthless. What is in the medical facility, that is the only thing worth having."

"What are you doing?" Najan's confused gaze shifted to Varsha's face.

"Handling the business you should have the first time." Varsha released a bitter laugh. "A woman handling a man's job."

"What will killing me do?" Khalil said in a tone that was too calm for the moment at hand. "The new Kings are in play, you cannot …"

"I told Najan a dead man cannot contest the authenticity of his signature. By the time the Kings are done grieving you and the loss of their women, it will be too late." Varsha stepped mere inches from Khalil with an evil snarl that marred the beauty of her face. "I will have a piece of what you loved so much and it will come in the form of taking the biggest and most profitable segment of the Castle. Remember, I was the one who suggested Dr. Fowler in the first place." Varsha snatched the paperwork from the desk.

"And that is because he was your lover, right?"

Varsha staggered backward. "Wait … you."

"Of course. The man you were sneaking around to sleep with all of these years." Khalil sighed and there was a world of weariness in that sound. "As long as he did the honors, it meant I never had to soil myself by being intimate with you. He did me a solid. Well, until he became greedy."

Tiffany exchanged appalled looks with Skyler as an armed man in a grey suit moved passed the chairs until he stood next to Varsha. Tiffany glanced at Skyler whose hand was slid into her crossbody bag. She scanned the room. Eleven against four. The odds weren't in their favor.

Cameron inserted herself between Khalil and Varsha.

"Are you willing to die for this man?" Varsha huffed in Cameron's face.

"From the sounds of it, you're really not giving us much of a choice," Tiffany injected causing Varsha to send a deadly look her way.

"Handle this." She touched the shoulder of the man in the grey suit. "No one." Varsha glanced at Najan. "No one leaves alive and find Aashna when you're done here."

"Tiffany shield up," Cameron yelled.

Tiffany dropped the device to the ground and it expanded seven feet in height and quadrupled in width as Skyler moved to her side. Cameron spun Khalil toward her, pulling him behind the shield as the bullets began to fly. Tiffany's body stilled as bullets pinged off the clear wall of protection. Skyler shot back from beyond the shield causing Najan to dive for cover behind the nearest chair. Cameron fired and four bodies hit the ground.

Khalil turned his back to Tiffany. "Please take these off my hands."

"Not so fast." Cameron shifted her body blocking Varsha's escape. Two men tried to grab Cameron. She released her hold on Varsha, slamming her elbow into the jaw of one of the assailants.

"Tiffany concentrate," Khalil's voice snapped her focus away from Cameron. "I need these off to help her."

The hail of bullets temporarily stopped as the men reloaded. Najan took the opportunity to race out of the door with Skyler on his tail.

Tiffany jammed her hand into the crossbody, pulling out the pen similar to the one Zuri had been given. She was careful to cut the ties without nicking his skin.

When Tiffany glanced up, Varsha was gone. All but two men were on the floor. Cameron kicked a man over one of the wing back chairs then slammed a golden spear across the face of the other. Khalil, gripped Tiffany's hand and took off toward the hidden entrance. She pulled out the Ruger, following him into the dark passage. Two light beams came at them in the darkest part of the tunnel to reveal Varsha being walked back in by Milan and Temple at gun point.

"It seems someone was trying to slip away from the party early," Milan said.

Skyler returned with a limping Najan. Dwayne and the Kings entered the study seconds later with their weapons drawn. They surveyed the area, then lowered their guns with relief clearly displayed on their faces.

Khalil's gaze flickered between Najan and Varsha. "You thought you would take me and my wife out while the Kings were otherwise occupied." He swept a gaze across the women in the room and smiled. "You forgot, the most powerful piece on a chessboard is ... the queen."

CHAPTER 32

"We're here today to show a little love to a man with a master plan," Ellen DeGeneres said on the monitor Miguel and Dwayne were watching from backstage. "He's an educator who founded a school that is certainly a place I wish was available when I was in junior high. Check this out."

The screen behind her zoomed in on the outside of Excel's steel, brick and glass structure. Miguel's freshly scrubbed face appeared onscreen. "Hi. I'm Miguel Ramos and I'm going to take you on a little tour of my second home."

The virtual tour walked through all aspects of Excel Charter School. All of America saw the offices that served as classrooms, the boardrooms where group projects and discussions were held, the math and science labs, the arts and music emporium, physical education area, the computer lab, and the extensive library.

Ellen's audience gave a rousing round of applause when Miguel showed them the full service restaurant. They went wild with claps and cheers when he showed them the day's meal choices of steak and potatoes, grilled salmon and asparagus, or vegan wraps and hummus, all served on China, with full silverware and cloth napkins.

"No sodas or fast food up in this camp," Miguel said, wiggling his eyebrows.

The audience laughed.

"But let me introduce you to the man who started it all," he said walking past the receptionist and the office staff to get to Dwayne's office. He knocked once and opened the door when he heard, "Enter."

Miguel swept in with the camera crews in tow. He glanced down at the salad on the desk near the keyboard and said, "What's up, Doc?"

Dwayne's gaze narrowed at him, but then he took notice of the carrots on top of all the greenery on his plate and said, "Ah, you've got jokes."

The audience laughed as the screen went black.

Ellen stood and said, "I'd like to welcome Dwayne Harper and Miguel Ramos to the *Ellen* show."

The applause was deafening as everyone stood to greet the two who walked out from behind the curtain and made their way over to the chairs next to Ellen, who embraced them both.

"Well, tell us the motivation behind Excel."

Dwayne shared about Khalil Germaine and attending Macro International growing up. He told about the men who were fellow scholars and how they had achieved great levels of success, but were now focused on more humanitarian endeavors.

"And I understand there was a bit of controversy this past year …" Ellen hedged.

Miguel filled her in about the drama surrounding the school's opposition, and what happened with the seniors and how the scholars first worked to help them, then the Knights and Kings became involved. He told of the outcome, and the audience "oohed" and "aahed" as images displayed behind them giving, a pictorial of what had been accomplished.

"And part of the reason Mr. Sanchez was so against all the good works that Dwayne was doing was that he didn't want him to find favor with our community," Miguel said. "That backfired big time."

He put a sly glance in Dwayne's direction. "Personally, I think Mr. Harper would do a better job as alderman than Mr. Sanchez ever did."

"I'm not …" Dwayne shook his head and gave Miguel a warning glare, which Miguel totally ignored. "That is not my thing. Education. That's my wheel house."

"Helping people, helping the community," Miguel shot back, his tone somber. "I thought that was in your wheelhouse, too."

"Well," Ellen said, nodding. "On that note, maybe this time next year we'll be seeing the name Alderman Dwayne Harper."

Miguel stood, clapping so enthusiastically that the audience and Ellen laughed.

The one person who didn't share the zeal was Dwayne, who gave both Ellen and Miguel the side eye.

CHAPTER 33

"Did you see the latest numbers, Mr. Harper?" Geo asked Dwayne, pointing to a newscaster on the screen.

"I'm a little too nervous to look right now," Dwayne replied, raising his chin to accept a kiss from Tiffany.

"You're going to do just fine," she said. "With all the people you have pulling for you"—she waved her hand in the air with a flourish—"you can't lose."

A year had passed, one which had probably been the most trying of Dwayne's life. But he thanked God that things were working out.

Miguel, his mother, and his sister, now resided in one of Jai's rental properties. Ms. Ramos had availed herself of the online adult classes at Excel to improve her skillset while working as an assistant at the Castle.

His sister had not given birth yet. But she had vowed not to quit school because of the baby. With the help of Dwayne and his sister Val, she was lining up resources like subsidized daycare so she could continue her education while being a parent.

Much to Dwayne's delight, the situation with Miguel and Eduardo had been resolved without any bloodshed. Daron and Dro had taken Eduardo to task for his attempts to use the newfound relationship and vulnerability to manipulate Miguel. That discussion had ended with a warning from Dwayne. "Come near him or his family again, I'll put a bullet in you myself. You won't have to worry about prison. They won't find your body until I'm in my own grave."

Eduardo must have believed they would carry out that plan. No one had heard a peep about it. And then, Miguel had taken his mother in to the police and played the recording he had kept on his phone. Though there was a statute of limitations on rape, there was not one on filing the charges, getting the recording submitted into evidence, then filing a civil lawsuit to take Sanchez for every dime he had.

Now here Dwayne was running for Alderman.

Miguel and his fellow scholars had spearheaded Dwayne's campaign. They'd taken the initiative to canvas the neighborhood with their parents and some of the seniors in his Abuelita's building, collecting signatures for his write-in candidacy. Scholars interested in political science had done research on the most effective type of campaign to run. Excel's marketing and advertising majors had handled the press releases, public appearances, and content for commercials.

Scholars majoring in finance took the helm in the fundraising efforts. Excel's computer gurus designed websites, mailing list campaigns, podcasts, and social media platforms to get across to the voting public the ideals Dwayne stood for.

Other scholars manned the telephone banks along with seniors from Serenity Place. But even with young and old working together, Dwayne wasn't a shoo-in for the position of Alderman. Eduardo Sanchez still had the connections and ability to use dirty tricks to get his way. His efforts at voter intimidation, outright bribing, trying to purge the voter rolls, wasn't as successful as he had hoped. All the more reason why every single vote mattered to Dwayne.

The community had all but demanded that Dwayne run for alderman after Lola Sanders' public relations firm publicized how the scholars' actions had led to the State coming in and stripping Caesar Wilson of the subsidized funding he received for Serenity House. The hefty fines levied against him would keep him in the State's debt for the next fifty years. The Kings took over the building and its management, along with several others that were in Wilson's purview.

Uncle Bubba and Greta came to the long rectangular table where Dwayne and Tiffany were seated. "Nephew, I'm really proud of you."

"Look, he's blushing," Tiffany teased, rubbing Dwayne's cheek.

Dwayne clinked a pen on his water glass to get everyone's attention. "Gather around please." The excited chatter in the room diminished.

Reno and Dro whistled and clapped wildly from their corner of the room. "Speech," they shouted.

Dwayne looked around the room at his many friends. "I don't know what the outcome of the voting will be. But I just want to say that I feel so blessed to have had each of you behind me—even though you had to drag me kicking and screaming to cast my hat in the race."

The crowd laughed.

"But seriously, I couldn't have done any of this without you." He put his fist to chest, then pointed at his fellow Kings and Knights—minus Dro, Daron and Jai. "Those are my brothers right there. I'm surrounded by greatness."

The men took shy bows when the crowd cheered them on.

"These men purchased and rehabbed Serenity House after the courts finished taking Caesar Wilson through the wringer for how he'd treated our seniors."

Someone from the audience yelled, "And he's in jail, where he belongs."

The audience cheered.

Another supporter cupped his hands around his mouth and shouted,

"And by the time he pays all the fines the City hit him with, he won't have any money left."

Another roar of approval from the crowd.

The Pastor and his wife who allowed Eduardo to connive against the elders were relieved of their church, and for the time being the membership was being pastored by a Pastor Tony Baltimore and his wife, Kari.

Dwayne waited for the crowd to grow quiet before he spoke again. "What a lot of you don't know is that after my brother Kings took over Serenity House, they insisted that the Serenity House tenants live at the Castle while Serenity House was gutted and rebuilt." He paced the area in front of the table. "And after the seniors were able to move back into Serenity House, my fellow King Jai made arrangements for them to have medical personnel onsite around the clock and other services and resources they would need."

Miguel's grandmother and the other female tenants blew kisses at Dwayne, Grant, Reno, Shaz, Vikkas, and Khalil. The seniors flourished under all the attention that had been showered on them. The gifts of handcrafted items and homemade dishes were a welcome thing. Shaz especially loved to be on the receiving end of the latter.

Dwayne continued. "These young people that you see in this room put this campaign together and just about ran it by themselves. I'm surrounded by greatness."

All around the room, Miguel and his classmates stood at attention and tipped imaginary hats in Dwayne's direction.

"My Uncle's over there. That man has been my rock since I was knee-high to a duck," he said with a chuckle. "I'm surrounded by greatness."

Uncle Bubba pointed at Dwayne and gave a big smile.

"That's his beautiful bride Greta. Love you, auntie." He searched the room, then added, "My twin sister, Val, is right there, along with her husband Hunter, and their son Caleb. Family means everything to me. I'm surrounded by greatness."

Val leaned into her husband's arms, beaming at her brother.

He looked down at Tiffany, who was seated at the table where he stood. "To my fiancé, Tiffany. You make me feel I can do anything. I'm surrounded by greatness."

She dabbed at her eyes with a lacy handkerchief.

Laying eyes on Sophia brought back memories of the accusations surrounding the parenting classes he attended with her. Val had helped Sophia to heal emotionally from the abuse and to set off on the path of making better life choices. His fellow King, Shaz, had successfully represented her in the court battle to clear her name and get her child back. The father was still dragging her through court to fight against the massive amount of child support Shaz was able to secure.

"I don't know if there's any other man in the world who is as blessed as—"

"Hey, hold up," one of the lookers-on demanded, gesturing to the television. "They're about to announce the results. Turn that up."

Dwayne held his breath and listened to Cheryl Burton who first introduced a little of the neighborhood's drama and background. She ended with, "The final tallies are now in for the local positions." Her smile widened. "Lawndale will seat a new alderman. Dwayne Harper won by a landslide, ousting longtime incumbent Eduardo Sanchez."

A victory roar went up from everyone. Friends and family immediately surrounded Dwayne who embraced everyone and thanked them. Then he moved to the center of the room, faced the people who had taken this journey with him and said, "Like I said, I'm surrounded by greatness."

* * *

Tiffany took another sip of champagne and lifted her glass in toast to Dwayne. Sudden movement at the door caught her attention. Her breathing hitched the moment Daron, Dro, and Jai walked in with a teenager who had an anxious expression as she scanned the many faces of the people congregated across several connected areas.

Tiffany searched Dwayne's eyes for a moment. Her lips parted to speak but no words would come.

Grant and Shaz moved forward to flank Tiffany on each side, hooking their arms under hers and guiding her toward the entrance. Twice, her knees nearly buckled with an emotion she couldn't name. She glanced over her shoulder at Dwayne, who nodded, smiled, and gestured for her to keep moving.

A few feet away from the young girl who was nearly her spitting image, the tears came without any signs of ceasing any time soon. The girl left her escort's side and covered those last feet on her own, throwing her arms around Tiffany, who was still so in shock it took a few seconds for her to return the embrace.

"They told me this wonderful story," she whispered into Tiffany's ear. "They say that you're my real mother." She pulled away to look into Tiffany's eyes.

Tiffany's hands reached up, cupping the youngster's face in her hands. "They don't have to say," she answered. "I know I'm your mother."

EPILOGUE

"Dearly beloved we are gathered here today …," Khalil said, smiling at the nine men around the table.

"To get through this thing called life," Dro teased, shaking his head at the reference to a song titled *Let's Go Crazy*. "Aaaaaaaand Khalil's a Prince fan, too."

"Um, no. James Brown is his favorite," Dwayne countered, leaning back in his chair as he grinned. "Quotes him all the time."

"Well, he is the godfather of soul," Khalil offered, taking the seat at the newly situated boardroom table that was in an area that once housed the library and study. Turning serious, he said, "I'm proud to announce that all Castle operations will now be handled from this mission control center. We started in the maze in the basement because when plans are being formulated, we must treat them like a pregnancy. Only when the plans start showing, do you start telling. And you only share it with ones who can support your vision." Khalil looked over to Grant. "The floor is yours."

"Brothers, here are the plans for the eight schools that will open within the year," Grant said, pressing the remote to display the architectural designs on the screen behind them. "Reno and I, with direct insight from Dwayne, have put in a lot of hours to create building standards that will meet not only CPS standards, but our own."

Reno left his chair and walked around the table until he stood next to Grant. "We'll decide today whether each school will be named after the King himself or the area where he was raised, but all designations will be International Magnet School. The curriculum and operation guidelines will be as Dwayne has created, and the initial focus on each student will be on how they learn as well as what they learn. That has been the key to Macro's and now, Excel's, success."

"How many students will each school hold?" Vikkas asked.

Khalil tapped his finger on a sheet that outlined the strategic plan. "One hundred-eighty. Twenty sets of nine scholars each. Twenty boardrooms, twenty clusters. Everything else mirrors Excel and Macro all the way down the line."

"Will this be enough?" Jai asked, sweeping a gaze across the men in the room. "There are millions of teens in Chicago alone. Nine schools are not going to address the issues of an inclusive education that will prepare them for success."

"This is only the beginning," Khalil said. "But it has to start somewhere. And I am truly grateful that it starts with you." Khalil stood, then paced the open areas surrounding the table. "I have been reaching out to other former scholars of Macro. And I will continue with my bi-monthly meetings with your beloveds. You will need help from people who understand what you're trying to achieve. You have already understood exactly what my mission entailed."

He aimed the remote and it changed to images of a poverty-stricken family, then to a little girl crying, holding onto a little boy, and on to other photos that expressed many facets of the world's sad conditions. "There is so much pain and suffering in the world that so many have given up hope. Most are looking to religious leaders and politicians to solve the problems, but the answer lies within. We cannot wait for them to do what is best for us. We have to do it." Khalil placed a gaze on each one of them. "The answer has always resided first within the individual, then the team, then outward from there."

Khalil glanced at Jai, who had already broken ground for construction on eight other healing centers headed by the Knights, Tiffany Harper, and Jennifer—who had also recruited several other nurses from the maternity floor that cared for Temple Maharaj during her time at Meridian. He placed a hand on Daron's shoulder.

Daron reached up to place his hand over Khalil's as he smiled. His education center would focus on Science, Technology, and Inventions, and they would also target disadvantaged youth, taking them in and giving them a better path before the streets claimed them.

"And this had nothing to do with religion," Khalil continued. "That is the thing that my family never understood." He gestured to Reno. "You are Catholic." Then to Dwayne, Shaz and Kaleb. "Non-denominational Christians." To Jai, then Vikkas. "Baha'i. Each of you embraces a different belief. But look at how we came together to do something positive for man and womankind. That comes from the heart."

His gaze narrowed on Shaz. "I understand that your school focuses on fitness, food service and hospitality industries," Khalil said with a chuckle.

Shaz leaned back in his chair, rubbed his tight abs. "Indeed, and I'm going to make sure there's a Jamaican restaurant up in that camp."

"Yes, but you might want to make sure there is enough left for everyone else, eh?"

The men roared with laughter as Shaz threw up his hands and said, "See, why you want to bring up old stuff."

"I have a question," Dro said, as the laughter tamped down. "Khalil …"

"Yes, my son."

"The night that you were shot ..." Dro flickered a gaze at Daron, who nodded for him to continue. "You angled and put yourself into position ... before the first shot was even fired."

Vikkas stiffened and his head whipped to his father.

"You knew they were coming," Daron added. "Five shots landed, three were deflected. How?"

Khalil surveyed the expectant faces of the men at the table. He slowly unbuttoned his customary white tunic to reveal a silver medallion that held a crafted image of each man currently sitting at the table.

Three of the bullets were still lodged in the place where Daron, Grant, and Dwayne's images had been etched. Two holes were in the spot where Shaz and Jai's image rested. The medallion was suspended from a silver chain that rested just above Khalil's heart.

The tunic also revealed that he now wore a holstered weapon of his own. Daron and Dro shared a glance and an appreciative nod.

"Nothing can take you from this earth if God wills that your reason for being here is not done."

Dwayne pointed to the weapon, chuckled at first, then released an outright laugh. "Like Khalil taught us: Peace when feasible. Kick ass and take names when necessary."

"Amen to that, my son," Khalil whispered. "Amen to that. Know that as we stand together as Kings of the Castle, we will leave an indelible impression on this earth. Even the Bible says that the meek shall inherit the earth." Then he smiled. "But that does not mean we have to be sitting ducks in the process."

Excerpt from
NO RIGHT WAY
TO DO A WRONG THING
by Janice M. Allen

"I know you're not walking around in broad daylight with a shotgun," Val gasped.

Uncle Bubba stopped on the porch and leaned on his cane, holding the gun out just as calmly as he might hold out a piece of candy to a starry-eyed child. "It ain't real, Val."

She caught his arm and yanked him inside the house, scanning the area to see if any neighbors were nearby. "It's real enough to get you shot if the police see you with it."

"And it's real enough to keep that husband of yours in line if he comes back here actin' a fool," Uncle Bubba replied. He laid it across the coffee table, letting the heavy metal barrel clink a little too hard against the glass. "I used to respect that boy, but I swear I don't know what's gotten into him. I betcha if I put some lead in him though, that'll tighten him up real good. Get his head on straight."

Her twin brother Dwayne walked in the front door, arms loaded with overnight bags and a carry-out box that said Beggars Pizza.

"And you," Val scolded as Dwayne kicked the door closed. "Why'd you let Uncle Bubba come out of the house with that thing?" She tossed a cold glance at the shotgun.

"Take it in the other room if you don't want to see it," Uncle Bubba ordered.

"I'll keep a close eye on him," Dwayne promised. "He can't hurt anybody with it anyway unless he uses it to beat them over the head."

Uncle Bubba nodded. "Yeah, that gets my vote." He snickered as he eased down on the couch. "Dwayne, put that stuff down and get that Bad Boys DVD out of my bag." He patted the couch cushion. "Val, come watch it with me. You need to relax."

Dwayne sat the bags on the dining room table and brought the pizza into the living room. "Get a whiff of this," he said to Val as he opened the lid and fanned the steam toward her.

Val covered her nose and jerked her head the other way. "It's making me nauseous." She pushed the box away.

"I'm sorry, li'l sis. I guess I have to get used to you being pregnant." He took the box in the dining room and came back with the movie.

"You're not too sick to sit with me, are ya?" Uncle Bubba asked Val as Dwayne loaded the DVD player.

She laid a hand on her stomach, trying to settle the queasiness. "No, Uncle Bubba. That, I can do."

"I'm going to have some pizza," Dwayne said as he headed toward the kitchen.

Uncle Bubba scooted over, and Val curled up beside him. Her head settled on his shoulder and she prayed that peace would tiptoe into her soul.

מ מ מ

Val awoke two hours later to a room that was completely dark except for the brightness of the screen on the sixty-inch plasma tv. She lifted her head from Uncle Bubba's shoulder and fluffed her hair where it had gotten flat while she slept.

"Told you that you needed to rest," he said, patting her gently on the arm. "You didn't slobber on me, did you?" He inspected his sleeve.

She gave him a playful nudge with her shoulder, then pried herself off of the sofa and stretched. Headlights in the driveway and the unmistakable hum of her husband's SUV made her whole body tense up. Suddenly she found it hard to breathe.

Kurt. Dwayne. Uncle Bubba. The shotgun.

Nothing but trouble waiting to happen.

Uncle Bubba called for Dwayne. "Come down here, boy, and pass me my piece."

Dwayne's footsteps clattered overhead, followed by him rushing down the stairs. "I thought you said forty-eight hours," he said to Val as he made it to the landing.

"The police said forty-eight hours," she corrected.

"Not only is the man unable to tell his wife from another woman, but he can't tell time either," Uncle Bubba grumbled as Dwayne rounded the corner. Dwayne went straight for the shotgun. Val went straight for the cordless phone in the kitchen.

"I'm calling the police," she said, scurrying back to the living room the moment Kurt's key slid in the first of the two locked doors.

Uncle Bubba grunted with the effort to get off of the couch. "Val, put the phone down," he said in a muffled tone. "We got this under control."

She shivered but relented, her hands shaking as she laid the phone on the love seat. "Uncle Bubba, that is just a toy gun, right?" she whispered back.

He didn't bother to answer.

Dwayne took up a position behind the door. Val stood frozen in place, praying that yellow crime scene tape wouldn't soon decorate her home.

The last lock clicked and Kurt tipped into the semi-dark house. "Now look, Val, I don't want any trouble," he said as he felt for the switch on the wall. "I just need to get my—"

Uncle Bubba cleared his throat as soon as the decorative ceiling light came on. Kurt's gaze traveled from the old man to the shotgun he held at his side. Dwayne stepped from behind the door. Kurt glared at the two men like they were bullies on the playground. "Did you have to get involved in our business?"

Dwayne positioned himself protectively in front of Val. "My sister is my business." He gestured to the rest of the house. "The police having to come to this camp is our business."

Peeking around Dwayne's sturdy body, Val asked, "Why are you here?"

Kurt's gaze remained locked on Dwayne.

"You heard the girl," Uncle Bubba prodded. "What do you want?"

"I just needed to get a few things," Kurt said, his gaze darting around the room, probably trying to find some object to protect himself with.

"Well, me and Dwayne here are gonna do you like the cops prob'ly did you," Uncle Bubba advised. "We gonna escort you through the house so you can grab what you need and get to steppin'."

Dwayne took a few steps forward and reached for Kurt's elbow. Kurt wrenched away. "Man, don't put your hands on me. This is my house," he said, clenching his teeth and thumping his chest with his index finger.

"You wait one cotton-pickin' minute," Uncle Bubba said, raising the stock of the shotgun to his shoulder and cocking the pump action.

All sound left the room.

Val's legs felt as though they were dissolving under her own weight. But she wouldn't give Kurt the satisfaction of seeing her blatant terror. She jutted her chin out and crossed her arms, matching Dwayne's stance.

A car door slammed outside. A few seconds later, the doorbell rang.

"Mama, I thought I told you to stay in the truck," Kurt answered without turning to face the door.

"She your bodyguard now?" Uncle Bubba taunted, the barrel still aimed at Kurt.

"Is everything all right, son?" Kurt's mother asked through the door. There was a slight, dull bump on the door as if she had pressed her head against it to listen in on what was happening inside.

"He'll be right out, Mama Melva," Val said loudly, motioning for Dwayne to hurry up and take Kurt to get his stuff so he could leave. A brisk burst of air swept over Val as the two men rushed past her. Uncle Bubba brought up the rear, his "phony" shotgun still trained on Kurt.

Mrs. Timmons' footsteps crossed the porch, clicked along the sidewalk, and then the SUV door opened and closed.

Three minutes later, Val's guardian angels were ushering Kurt to the front door. A laptop was in his left hand. With the other hand, he hung onto a pair of dress shoes with black socks stuffed in them. Two shirts and two pairs of slacks still on the hangers were draped over his right arm. The shaving kit, toothbrush and clean underwear sitting atop the pants and shirts were poised to slide to the floor. He jostled his belongings, trying to open the front door.

Dwayne opened it for him, saying "We're gonna be here for a hot minute, so don't think about coming back and starting some mess."

Looking like a ram ready to butt heads with a rival male, Kurt barged past his brother-in-law.

Having to have the last word, Uncle Bubba said, "You heard my nephew. Don't start none, won't be none!" As he closed the door, he crooned, "Bad boys, bad boys, whatcha gonna do? Whatcha gonna do when they come for you?"

Get your copy of No Right Way Today!

EXCERPT FROM CAYENNE
by Janice M. Allen

Michael raised the trunk and gazed at his ex-girlfriend's unconscious body. Nia was blindfolded, her wrists and ankles bloodied by the thick rope binding them. He had to play his cards just right if he intended to get her out of this alive.

"You sure nobody saw you snatch her?" Michael asked Lee as the self-proclaimed pretty boy and wannabe gangster got out of his car.

"Positive." Lee leaned over to admire his expertly trimmed goatee in the side view mirror.

Michael had sworn to himself that Nia wouldn't slip through his fingers ever again. He would make things right this time, make her his wife—as soon as he could free her from her captors.

"Before Angelique kills sleeping beauty," Lee said, "I'm gonna break her off some of what all the women beg me for." He gave a wicked sneer that set Michael's nerves on edge.

Though his fists were aching to have a long conversation with Lee's face, Michael chomped down on his anger. *Months of undercover work will go down the drain if I lose my cool. Just roll with the situation.*

"What you'd better do is jump back in the car and meet up with your sister like she told you to," Michael warned. "You know how antsy people can get in the middle of this kind of deal." He glanced at his watch, wishing Lee wasn't so lax about the process. "Keep them waiting, and they'll get cold feet and back out. Then there won't be a baby to sell, and word will get out that Angelique can't deliver on her promises. She'll be pissed if that happens."

"Maaan, you think I'm scared of that chick?" Lee's chest was stuck out like a rooster in a cockfight, but his voice sounded more like a hen with its neck on the chopping block. "My sister don't run things. I do."

Truthfully, the only thing Lee ran was his mouth. None of the informants Michael had encountered in his ten years of undercover work had ever divulged as much information as Lee belched out while bragging about his power, prowess, prosperity, and plans—none of which he possessed. Angelique was the brains behind everything they did, even the plan to cash in on the child trafficking business.

Michael raised his hands in mock surrender. "I hear you loud and clear. You call the shots. So how about I look after her"—he nodded toward Nia—"until you get back?"

Cursing under his breath, Lee motioned for Michael to remove Nia from the confines of his shiny black 2018 Lexus RX.

Bending his six-four frame down toward the open trunk, Michael gathered her in his arms, then laid her slender body across his shoulder.

"She woke up and started makin' noises while I was on the road," Lee said as he transferred Nia's purse from his vehicle to a hook on the wall. "So I pulled over and put that rag on her face again." He slammed the trunk down and gave a two-finger wave.

When Michael opened the garage door of Angelique's secluded Bella Vista, Illinois estate, Lee sped off into the night.

Nia never flinched. Her breathing remained slow and steady as the door closed, shutting her off from the rest of the outside world.

Not knowing when Lee and Angelique would return, getting Nia out of that place was Michael's first priority. But his concerns about Nia being unconscious for three hours or more trumped that. Shifting her body so that she was cradled against his chest, Michael carried Nia to his Cadillac CTS and laid her across the back seat, propping her head and shoulders against the passenger door.

Her natural beauty mesmerized him as always. Baby-soft caramel-colored skin was the canvas for eyebrows that framed her brown eyes like they were works of art. Thick black hair created a halo around her face. Sensuously-curved lips begged for his attention. He placed a feather-light kiss on them.

In a fairy tale, she would awaken with undying gratitude and admiration toward him. In real life, only smelling salts would revive her. And he feared that no amount of magic kisses or potions could ever make her regard him favorably again.

Michael extracted a bottle of smelling salts from the first aid kit he kept in the car. Getting in the driver's seat, he angled his body toward Nia and waved the bottle several inches away from her nose.

She wrenched away from the acrid smell of ammonia, her body convulsing with coughs.

He could only imagine the disorientation she felt as she slowly came to her senses. She thrashed around, trying to free her hands, take the blindfold off, and possibly make a run for it. If the tables were turned, flight would've been the first thing on his mind too.

Putting a hand to her chest, he gently held her in place. The heartbeat that was faint as he held her against his chest a moment ago now pounded against his palm like a battering ram.

"Shhh," he whispered.

Her head darted around to follow his hushed tone, then to take in other sounds in the space: a dog barking in a nearby yard; the hum of the furnace coming to life in the adjoining utility room; his ragged breathing slowing down as the fear of losing her to killers subsided.

Michael braced himself, knowing that once he said something she would recognize him. "I'm going to take off your blindfold."

She gasped, cringed, and craned her head toward the sound of his voice.

He gently slid a hand under her head. Fighting the urge to massage away the tension and anxiety he felt in the taut muscles at the nape of her neck, he lifted her head and untied the black triangular bandana that covered her eyes and hung down to her chin. It slipped off, revealing another gag Lee had placed in her mouth.

Did it really take all this?

With the blindfold off, light spilling from the dome light directly over Nia's head caused her to squint for a split second. When she fully opened her eyes, she honed in on Michael's face. Her expression transformed from bewilderment to disgust and horror, giving voice to everything she couldn't vocalize.

Why did you do this to me?!

Get your copy of Cayenne today.

Janice M. Allen

National Bestselling Author, Janice M. Allen, is living proof that it's never too late to grow and blossom. She uncovered her gift of writing in 2014 when she co-authored *Baring It All: The Ins and Outs of Publishing*, a self-help manual for writers.

Her foray into fiction began with her first novel, *No Right Way to do a Wrong Thing*, which was released in 2018 and became an AALBC bestseller. She followed that with the short story Cayenne.

Janice and eight other authors collaborated to co-write a romance novel called *Kings of the Castle*, published in November 2019. Janice's novel King of Lawndale is one of eight follow-up novels released in that series.

Janice plans to publish two Christian inspirational books in 2020.

Newly married to Pastor Sammie Allen, Janice resides in Ridgecrest, California.

Learn more at
www.janicemallen.com
https://www.facebook.com/AuthorJaniceMAllen
https://www.facebook.com/janice.allen123

About the kings of the castle series

Books 2-9 are standalones, no cliffhangers, and can be read in any order.

Book 1 – Kings of the Castle, the introduction to the series and story of King of Wilmette (Vikkas Germaine)

USA TODAY, New York Times, and National Bestselling Authors work together to provide you with a world you'll never want to leave. The Castle. Powerful men unexpectedly brought together by their pasts and current circumstances will become a force to be reckoned with. Their combined efforts to find the people responsible for the attempt on their mentor's life, is the beginning of dangerous challenges that will alter the path of their lives forever. Not to mention, they will also draw the ire and deadly intent of current Castle members who wield major influence across the globe.

Fate made them brothers, but protecting the Castle and the women they love, will make them Kings. www.thekingsofthecastle.com

King of Chatham - Book 2 - Reno
King of Evanston - Book 3 - Shaz
King of Devon - Book 4 - Jai
King of Morgan Park - Book 5 - Daron
King of South Shore - Book 6 - Kaleb
King of Lincoln Park - Book 7 - Grant
King of Hyde Park - Book 8 - Dro
King of Lawndale - Book 9 - Dwayne

Cover design by J. L. Woodson - www.woodsonstudio.com

About the kings of the castle series

Books 2-9 are standalones, no cliffhangers, and can be read in any order.

Book 1 – Kings of the Castle, the introduction to the series and story of King of Wilmette (Vikkas Germaine)

USA TODAY, New York Times, and National Bestselling Authors work together to provide you with a world you'll never want to leave. The Castle. Powerful men unexpectedly brought together by their pasts and current circumstances will become a force to be reckoned with. Their combined efforts to find the people responsible for the attempt on their mentor's life, is the beginning of dangerous challenges that will alter the path of their lives forever. Not to mention, they will also draw the ire and deadly intent of current Castle members who wield major influence across the globe.

Fate made them brothers, but protecting the Castle and the women they love, will make them Kings.

www.thekingsofthecastle.com

King of Chatham - Book 2

While Mariano "Reno" DeLuca uses his skills and resources to create safe havens for battered women, a surge in criminal activity within the Chatham area threatens the women's anonymity and security. When Zuri, an exotic Tanzanian Princess, arrives seeking refuge from an arranged marriage and its deadly consequences, Reno is now forced to relocate the women in the shelter, fend off unforeseen enemies of The Castle, and endeavor not to lose his heart to the mysterious woman.

King of Evanston - Book 3

Raised as an immigrant, he knows the heartache of family separation firsthand. His personal goals and business ethics collide when a vulnerable woman stands to lose her baby in an underhanded and profitable scheme crafted by powerful, ruthless businessmen and politicians who have nefarious ties to The Castle. Shaz and the Kings of the Castle collaborate to uproot the dark forces intent on changing the balance of power within The Castle and destroying their mentor. National Bestselling Author, J.L. Campbell presents book 3 in the Kings of the Castle Series, featuring Shaz Bostwick.

King of Devon - Book 4

When a coma patient becomes pregnant, Jaidev Maharaj's medical facility comes under a government microscope and media scrutiny. In the midst of the investigation, he receives a mysterious call from someone in his past that demands that more of him than he's ever been willing to give and is made aware of a dark family secret that will destroy the people he loves most.

King of Morgan Park - Book 5

Two things threaten to destroy several areas of Daron Kincaid's life—the tracking device he developed to locate victims of sex trafficking and an inherited membership in a mysterious outfit called The Castle. The new developments set the stage to dismantle the relationship with a woman who's been trained to make men weak or put them on the other side of the grave. The secrets Daron keeps from Cameron and his inner circle only complicates an already tumultuous situation caused by an FBI sting that brought down his former enemies. Can Daron take on his enemies, manage his secrets and loyalty to the Castle without permanently losing the woman he loves?

King of South Shore - Book 6

Award-winning real estate developer, Kaleb Valentine, is known for turning failing communities into thriving havens in the Metro Detroit area. His plans to rebuild his hometown neighborhood are dereailed with one phone call that puts Kaleb deep in the middle of an intense criminal investigation led by a detective who has a personal vendetta. Now he will have to deal with the ghosts of his past before they kill him.

King of Lincoln Park - Book 7

Grant Khambrel is a sexy, successful architect with big plans to expand his Texas Company. Unfortunately, a dark secret from his past could destroy it all unless he's willing to betray the man responsible for that success, and the woman who becomes the key to his salvation.

King of Hyde Park - Book 8

Alejandro "Dro" Reyes has been a "fixer" for as long as he could remember, which makes owning a crisis management company focused on repairing professional reputations the perfect fit. The same could be said of Lola Samuels, who is only vaguely aware of his "true" talents and seems to be oblivious to the growing attraction between them. His company, Vantage Point, is in high demand and business in the Windy City is booming. Until a mysterious call following an attempt on his mentor's life forces him to drop everything and accept a fated position with The Castle. But there's a hidden agenda and unexpected enemy that Alejandro doesn't see coming who threatens his life, his woman, and his throne.

King of Lawndale - Book 9

Dwayne Harper's passion is giving disadvantaged boys the tools to transform themselves into successful men. Unfortunately, the minute he steps up to take his place among the men he considers brothers, two things stand in his way: a political office that does not want the competition Dwayne's new education system will bring, and a well-connected former member of The Castle who will use everything in his power—even those who Dwayne mentors—to shut him down.

Author Bios

Naleighna Kai is the *USA TODAY* Bestselling Author of Every Woman Needs a Wife, Open Door Marriage, Loving Me for Me, Slaves of Heaven and several other controversial novels. She is founder of NK Tribe Called Success, The Cavalcade of Authors, and is a publishing and marketing consultant. www.naleighnakai.com

S. L. Jennings is a military wife, mom of three, coffee addict, Willy Wonka enthusiast, and real-life unicorn. She's also the New York Times and USA Today Bestselling author of Taint, Fear of Falling and the Se7en Sinners Series, along with a few other titles that she's too lazy to type. She's been with her high school sweetheart for almost twenty years, and he still can't get her Subway sandwich order right. But he's cute and brings her vodka, so she keeps him around. They currently reside in Spokane, WA with their three stinky boys and their equally stinky cat. www.sljenningsauthor.com

Martha Kennerson is the bestselling and award-winning author who's love of reading and writing is a significant part of who she is. She uses both to create the kinds of stories that touch the heart. Martha lives with her family in League City, Texas. She believes her current blessings are only matched by the struggle it took to achieve such happiness. To find out more about Martha and her journey, visit her website at www.marthakennerson.com and you can follow her on Facebook and Twitter.

J. L. Campbell is an award-winning Jamaican author who has written over thirty books in several romance subgenres. Campbell, who features Jamaican culture in her stories, is a certified editor, and also writes non-fiction. Visit her on the web at www.joylcampbell.com.

National bestselling author, **Lisa Watson**, is a native of Washington D.C., and writes in the Multicultural & Interracial, Contemporary, Romantic Suspense, and Sweet Romance genres. Her memorable novels for the Harlequin's Kimani line, The Match Broker series was listed as one of 2014's Top 25 Books of the Summer, and Top 50 Best Reads. Lisa lives in Raleigh, North Carolina with her husband of twenty-two years and two teenagers, and is avidly working on book one, Alexa King: The Guardian, in her second new Romantic Suspense series, The Lady Doyen and Book 2 in the Love and Danger Series. www.lisawatson.com

Karen D. Bradley is a national bestselling author and screenplay writer. English and Grammar were never her strongest subjects, but as life would have it, her weakest link would become her saving grace. Writing fiction became one of her favorite forms of therapy. She has penned several contemporary fiction, suspense, and romantic suspense novels. Visit Karen on the web at www.karendbradley.com

Janice M. Allen is a National Bestselling Author who has always been an avid reader of fiction. She even edited the work of other authors for several years. But she gets an incomparable thrill from creating stories that entertain readers and cause them to reflect on real life issues. No Right Way To Do A Wrong Thing is her first novel, followed by her short story Cayenne. www.janicemallen.com

London St. Charles has always had a passion for the pen, paper, and books. She is a Chicago native who uses the Windy City as a backdrop to the romance, suspense, and contemporary fiction stories she writes. London published her debut novel, The Husband We Share in 2017 and is one of nine authors in the anthology, Sugar. She also composes an online newsletter, London Writes, that keeps readers abreast of what's going on in her world. www.londonstcharles.com

MarZe Scott is a lifelong resident of Ypsilanti, Michigan and Graduate of University of Michigan. A lover of all things creative, MarZé enjoys reading, free-hand illustrating, jewelry making and makeup artistry.

Known for her vivid and captivating storytelling, MarZé has been writing short stories and poems since elementary school and developed a taste in high school for writing about provocative topics like the consequences of casual sex. You can find Gemini Rising, MarZé's debut novel, and short story Next Lifetime wherever books are sold. www.marzescott.com

Series mentors:

LaVerne Thompson is a *USA Today* Bestselling, award winning, multi-published author, an avid reader and a writer of contemporary, fantasy, and sci/fi sensual romances. She loves creating worlds within and without our world. She also writes romantic suspense and new adult romance under the pen name Ursula Sinclair also a USA Today Bestselling Author. www.lavernethompson.com

Kassanna is a strong believer in love at first sight and happily ever afters. Writing has always been her passion but fate sometimes has other roads that must first be taken .Navigating the road less traveled was not only unexpected but in the end extremely rewarding. Her books are mainly contemporary romance but she has delved into the paranormal, fantasy, and plans on expanding into other areas as the ideas come to her. Right now she is enjoying life and seeing her works come into fruition make it that much more pleasurable especially when her books make others smile. Kassanna wouldn't have it any other way. www.flavorfullove.com

CPSIA information can be obtained
at www.ICGtesting.com
Printed in the USA
LVHW090319100320
649433LV00006B/690